Return to the Ship of Dreams

Sinking the Unsinkable

Based on historical events

Courtney Morrow

Return to the Ship of Dreams: Sinking the Unsinkable

ISBN: 978-1-257-03130-6

Copyright © February 23, 2011

Published by Courtney Morrow, 8 Knightsbridge Ct., St. Peters, MO 63376.

Contents

Dedication

In memory of those lost at sea; their hearts will go on.

Author Note:

All events related strictly to the *Titanic* are based on historical events and are recreated to the best of the author's knowledge. Any and all mention of the movie *"Titanic"* and its characters, the show *"Dark Angel"* and its characters, and the movie *"Ghosts of the Abyss"* belongs in their entirety to James Cameron. Any mention of the movie *"Back to the Future"* belongs in its entirety to Steven Spielberg. Any songs and their lyrics are the property of the original artist and composer.

Introduction

This book you hold in your hands has been through its share of obstacles and troubles. It took over three years to write and publish, causing me much stress and grief. There were many times when I was sure I would not finish it. Fortunately, this bound copy proves me wrong.

Strangely enough, my fascination with the *Titanic* only began when I was eighteen. I had just graduated high school three months previously when my best friend—Sara Fehrmann, thank you very much for your contribution to this book—invited me to Branson, Missouri. While on our vacation, she and her family brought me to the *Titanic* museum. I had never really heard the whole story of the famed liner and never bothered to read into it. I had never even seen the movie.

Once inside, I was surprised by the story told from room to room. I had never really known that the ship was at sea for four whole, glorious days before it had struck an iceberg. I had also never known that it had sunk so slowly, spending almost three hours fighting to stay afloat. The story intrigued me at a level even I was not aware of yet. Once I returned home, I rented the movie, and the rest is history.

Over the next three years, I returned to the museum five more times, twice spending a grand total of four hours inside. I bought the movie, I bought books, I found blueprints, I bought a shirt, I bought the soundtrack, I bought a 3D puzzle, I bought a "Heart of the Ocean" necklace…I was obsessed.

Not long after watching the movie for the first time, I began thinking how cool it would be to be on the ship. My overactive imagination began to experiment with a time travel scenario.

Originally, I had a totally different idea for the story. I wanted the main character to be the great granddaughter of Jack and Rose. I wanted Rose to get pregnant, the child to be born as Jack, Jr., and for Rose to give the child up for adoption. Obviously, that idea did not go very far. It did not seem to be the right way to go. Instead, I came up with a far better idea.

I was walking through the museum my third time when I spotted a third-class exhibit. It was a suitcase that had been found in the water, containing only a blouse, purse and bracelet. The owner of the suitcase was unknown, but there were three initials on the side: "Z.F.A." At that moment, it was as though a light bulb lit in my head. The wheels began turning, the cogs began grinding, and the little typist sitting in my head began flying away at the keyboard. The idea that forms this very book began to come alive.

Many people I told about this book wondered why my character was not saving the *Titanic*. I believe that the story of the *Titanic* would not be as powerful if it had not sunk. Part of the power of the *Titanic*'s legend is the fact that it did sink.

History is full of life lessons for mankind. Name any tragedy or disaster that has ever happened, and I guarantee you that there was a lesson we learned from it.

If not for the 9/11 attacks, we would not have cracked down on airport security. If not for Hurricane Katrina, Gulf Coast residents would have still taken tropical storms for granted. If not for the sinking of the *Titanic*, mankind would have gone on thinking they were the most powerful thing in the universe, possibly leading to an even greater tragedy.

That is what history is: a series of life lessons that have bettered our way of life. You change that history, and you take away our very way of life.

For this reason, my story evolved the way it did. History should not be changed; it should be remembered.

It was such a joy to write this book. The story of the *Titanic* is one that never tires. Each time I read about it or see the movie, new ideas and feelings and emotions sprout into existence. It is as though I am seeing and hearing the story for the first time.

There were times when my mental computer shorted out, and my interest in the book faded. One of these writer's blocks lasted for four months. Eventually, my enthusiasm returned, and I went straight to work.

I'm sure you are tired of reading my thoughts and musings, and you want to get to the real story. However, I do have several people that it only seems fair I take the time to thank.

First of all, I would like to thank my God above, for without whose helping hand and creative mind, this book would not have been possible.

Second, I would very much like to thank James Cameron. His creative vision and passion for the *Titanic* led me to reach that level of story-telling. This book also would not have been possible without his film.

Third, I would like to thank my family. My mother Gwen and my father Steve always stood behind me one hundred percent. They encouraged me to reach for the stars, and it seems that I have reached beyond them. They and my sister Carrie were there every step of the way, listening to my tiresome explanations of what I was writing.

Fourth, I would like to thank my friends. Every day, they ask me when my book is going to be finished ("When can I proofread it for you?" "When is your book signing?" "When am I getting my free copy?"). It gave me a sense of accomplishment and gratitude at their excited emotions about my book. It gave me a real incentive to finish it. And a special thanks to my best friend Sara Fehrmann and my aunt Jo Hilliard. The two of them reviewed my book to help me finish it.

Fifth, I would especially like to thank you, my readers. I thank you for your interest in, not only the story of the *Titanic*, but for your interest in my book. As I write this acknowledgement, the book is nothing more than a document on my laptop. It seems strange to think that the people who read this very paragraph will be reading it from a book…with an actual cover and that new book smell. I can only send my deepest thanks to you for giving my book a shot.

And sixth, I would like to thank this book. It was my realization that writing is my first love that led to my change of career. Up until this point, I had been going into Nursing. Soon after finishing this book, I realized that I did not enjoy Nursing. I quickly switched to Theatre and have been enjoying it ever since. So, thank you, novel!

Well, enough of this dilly dallying! The suspense is killing you! Enjoy! Oh, and you're welcome.

Your author,
Courtney Morrow

1

Sweet Dreams

Ship's Log
April 10, 1912 – 12:00 p.m.
Titanic casts off from Southampton, England, and is towed towards the English Channel.
April 10, 1912 – 6:30 p.m.
Titanic docks at Cherbourg, France. 22 passengers disembark, cargo is unloaded, and 274 passengers board.
April 10, 1912 – 8:10 p.m.
Anchor is raised, and *Titanic* leaves France, heading around England's south coast.
April 11, 1912 – 11:30 a.m.

Titanic docks two miles from Queenstown, Ireland. 113 third-class passengers and 7 second-class passengers board with 1,385 mail bags. 7 people disembark.

April 11, 1912 – 1:30 p.m.

Starboard anchor is raised, and *Titanic* departs on her first Trans-Atlantic crossing for New York with 2,208 people onboard.

April 14, 1912 – 11:40 p.m.

Iceberg is spotted by Lookout Fleet about five hundred yards dead ahead. Fleet rings the warning bell three times and telephones the bridge: "Iceberg, right ahead!" Sixth Officer Moody acknowledges and relays to First Officer Murdoch, who calls: "Hard-a-starboard!" Murdoch orders engines stop and full astern. Murdoch activates the lever to close the watertight doors below. Helmsman spins the wheel "hard over." *Titanic* begins to veer to port, but the iceberg strikes the starboard bow and brushes along the ship. Thirty-seven seconds elapse from the sighting to the collision.

April 15, 1912 – 2:20 a.m.

Titanic sinks in the North Atlantic, killing 1,503 people due to shortage of lifeboats. *Carpathia* picks up the 705 survivors in the lifeboats and steams towards New York.

11

It sounds like the script for an epic tragedy film. But this tragedy is no fictional script; it is reality. It is the story of a ship destined for greatness, respect and notoriety. But, on its maiden voyage, it was stolen away from the world by a disaster that cannot be described by mere words. It was a disaster that changed the course of human history, a disaster that...Well, why don't you see for yourself...

~~

Pearl scrabbled up the smooth wood surface, fleeing for her very life. She gave a shriek as she slid down the deck and hit a wrought-iron bench. She immediately started crawling once again towards her destination; she **had** to get to the stern railing.

Pearl glanced quickly over her shoulder at the deadly water and became more resolved than ever to survive. She lunged for a handhold and miraculously caught something. She pulled herself along the deck, her lifejacket making it easier to slide. She looked at the white railing five feet away from her; she was almost to safety.

Pearl felt the ship start to angle upwards rapidly. She gave an almighty lunge and flung her hand out blindly. She gasped as her hand made contact with the cold metal. She pulled her arm forward and hooked her elbow through the bars. The stern was at a steep angle now and moving quickly.

Pearl glanced at the other doomed passengers left on the ship with her. Everyone was screaming and crying for help, but none would come. Not one of the fifteen hundred left onboard would live to see the sunrise. Pearl clamped her eyes shut against the scene, trying to block out the horrible reality. Tears began rolling down her cheeks as the cries of dying men, women and children rang in her ears.

Pearl felt her body leave the safety of the deck as the stern went vertical. Without the deck to support her, she had to let her elbow untangle from the railing and rely solely on her hands. Her fingers had grown numb from the cold, and she could barely hold on.

A deadly silence fell as the broken ship came to a rest. It bobbed like a cork as the people onboard clung for dear life. A few people lost their grip and fell, a sickening thud resounding as they hit railings and poles.

Pearl's fingers began to slip as she closed her eyes, praying a silent plea. Finally, she could not hold on any longer and began falling towards her watery grave...

~~

Pearl hit the floor and jolted awake. Her blankets tangled themselves around her body, and a cold sweat coated her skin. The ghost of a tear died on Pearl's cheek as the residual images lingered in her mind's eye.

Pearl lay beside her bed for several minutes, taking deep, rattling breaths.

It was all a dream, she thought as she put her face into her hands.

Little did she know that her dream was about to become a tragic reality...

2

Time Is Ours

Pearl made her way into the office, flipping the wavy, auburn hair that fell halfway down her upper arms back over her slender shoulder. She had always loved how her frame accentuated her: skinny, but not in an anorexic way.

Her deep green eyes wandered over the office as she passed by small exhibits of historical events. Each exhibit was a project their agency had worked on, and under the title was the name of the agent.

The Berlin Wall headed by Katrina Michelle...World War II headed by Sam Wyatt...Thomas Edison headed by Christopher Dean, and a few more.

Thirty-year-old Pearl Liberti worked at the Bureau for Historic Critical Accuracy, or the BHCA, located in downtown Manhattan, New York. They were the number one organization to go to for information. Unbeknownst to the public, the founder Kyle Tristan had discovered time travel. Some relative of his had left behind research papers about time travel, but his ancestor had never succeeded in manufacturing a practical application.

Kyle had gone through dozens of movies and books, trying to find the method that would work: *Back to the Future, Timeline, Terminator, The Time Machine* and even *Time Changers.* Finally, it took a combination of physics and movie magic to make it work. Turns out, Steven Spielberg had it pretty close when he made *Back to the Future.* Kyle succeeded in sending himself five minutes into the future. He then used that technology to build this institute, enabling the agents to go back in time and experience historical events for themselves.

They were contacted occasionally by authors writing biographies, people building museums and memorials, and many others. The BHCA picks an eligible candidate and sends him back to report on the selected event. In order to ensure the safety of the agents, they choose when to come back to the future. This ensures that they will not miss a rendezvous or possibly suffer a fatality.

Each agent is given a pendant that will bring them back at the holder's bidding. It works simply by holding the thumb on both sides of the pendant. It scans the thumbprint for security—we wouldn't want Hitler coming back from the dead—and brings the agent back to headquarters.

The BHCA, however, was not a big corporation, but a small agency that Pearl and seven of her friends founded ten years ago in 1995. The size of the agency was a key to the business; if they were not very well known, no one would find out about the time travel. However, they had all agreed that they could tell their families what they were doing.

Speaking of the team...

Their founder—and time travel inventor—was thirty-one-year-old Kyle Tristan. Kyle's short, jet-black hair and light blue eyes gave him an inquisitive appearance. And something about his smile—the way it reached all the way to his eyes, the depth of the smile, the dimples it created on his cheeks—gave him a purity of soul that was hard to come by.

Of course, being an inventor, Kyle was the group geek. The guy loved math and science, and could not get enough of it. Just think Egon Spengler from *Ghostbusters*, except maybe not so nerdy-looking. Kyle's good looks made up for his brains.

Twenty-eight-year-old Katrina Michelle was about as girly-girl as they come. She was the typical preppy cheerleader, but the black hair that fell to her elbows broke from the stereotypical blonde. At any hour of the day, one could see those big, brown eyes disappear behind a romance novel. That was her brand of poison: romance novels and chick flicks. Every day, her outfit contained something pink, whether it was her shirt or her nail polish.

Katrina had basically designated herself as the head designer, knowing her way around a needle and thread. She made most of her own clothes, so they figured, why not make costumes for the company?

Thirty-year-old Connor Jensen was born and raised in Texas. He was a pure Texan cowboy if there ever was one—spoke in a Texan accent, interested in country music like Willie Nelson, drove a full-size pick-up truck, and loved the Dallas Cowboys. His brown hair fell to the bottom of his ears, and his brown eyes were set on either side of a prominent nose. His strong brow and the set of his jaw were typical of his Irish background.

Connor was good with his hands and could build things, so he had been appointed as the mechanic. He had built the time machine, according to Kyle's specifications, and was in charge of repairing it and operating it.

Thirty-two-year-old Mary Gemini was the more old-fashioned one of them. She kept her blonde hair to her shoulders, and her blue eyes sparkled at everyone she saw. She was really into old seventies shows like *Dukes of Hazzard, Mork and Mindy* and *Starsky and Hutch*, and was often referred to as the mother of the group. Her fashion sense, however, did not suggest a mother at all. She had a knack for stringing a wardrobe together to create something stylish. For this reason, she worked with Katrina to design costumes for the period clothing of time traveling.

Twenty-nine-year-old Christopher Dean was the more down-to-earth persona of their operation. He was the shortest of the men, being only five-foot-seven, but the girls still thought he was tall. His short, brown hair and hazel eyes conveyed a sense of honesty. He enjoyed the more modern rock music, like Nickelback and Green Day. His movie genre of choice had remained horror movies since he could go see R-rated movies in the theatre. He especially loved the psychological thrillers like *The Shining, The Silence of the Lambs* and *Psycho*.

Chris worked in the records department. He had collected every book, journal, newspaper, document, video, blueprint, movie and picture in their library. The library contained every piece of information about every historical event needed to travel to any moment in time.

Thirty-year-old Rose Marie had to be the biggest tomboy any of them had ever seen. She kept her blonde hair only a few inches long, and her eyes were ferociously green. She tended to wear black a lot, but she definitely was not gothic. It was mostly dark colors, and she would never be caught dead in pink. She loved watching action movies, especially Bruce Willis and Harrison Ford ones. She always caught the Cowboys game with Connor.

Rose worked in the accounting department. Being good at finances, she kept track of their income and expenses, developing a company budget.

And thirty-two-year-old Sam Wyatt...What was there to say about Sam...Sam was the perfect guy. He was into all the same things as Pearl, and they loved hanging out with each other. He worked in public relations. He was the one interested parties contacted for business. He talked with prospective clients and even traveled to present their company to people.

Pearl, on the other hand, worked in the resources department. When given a new project, she would research clothing and any other accessories and supplies they might need for the trip. She then collaborated with Mary and Katrina for the costumes, Connor for the supplies, Rose for the cost of equipment, and Chris for the records they would need.

Pearl had joined her friends because she was a historian; she loved the stories of people from the past. Another reason she had joined being that her great grandparents had been aboard the *Titanic*. She was not sure if they had survived, but they did have a child with them on the voyage, so the baby obviously survived somehow. Someone had found Pearl's grandfather that night and put him up for adoption, and he had no clue whom his parents were.

Pearl's one wish before the business closed someday—if it ever did—was that they would do a project on *Titanic* and that she would get to go. Her best friend Sam shared her feelings; he had always been a big supporter of her dreams. He also shared her passion for the story of the *Titanic*.

Pearl entered her office and turned on her computer monitor. A message flashed on the screen that said:

One new e-mail message

Pearl opened it to see a message from Kyle.

MOVIE NIGHT TONIGHT AT SEVEN O'CLOCK

Pearl smiled as she marked the night on her calendar, looking forward to it.

~~

Pearl laughed as Connor fell from the couch. Kyle, who had pushed him off, quickly darted from the couch as Connor got to his feet. He chased Kyle around the room as the others laughed and doubled over.

Finally, Katrina stuck her foot out in front of Kyle, who promptly fell onto the floor. Connor jumped on him, wrestling as he pinned Kyle's arms to the floor.

"Everybody in!" Connor called, his dazzling smile lighting up as he stared at Kyle.

Kyle's eyes widened. "No!"

Katrina was the first to rush over and start tickling Kyle. He had always been extremely ticklish, and everyone knew it. Mary and Rose joined in as Kyle erupted in hysterical giggles.

"No!" Kyle gasped, shaking his head back and forth. "Stop!"

"What's the magic word?" Mary teased.

"Please!" Kyle fought out.

Katrina, Mary and Rose went back to the couch, and Connor let Kyle up.

"You guys are jerks," Kyle muttered as he walked to the snack bar and sat on one of the stools.

"Aw, you know you love us," said Chris from the couch next to Pearl. He had filled Kyle's vacated seat in the commotion.

The gang had a movie night together about once a month in the theatre room at Kyle's house. For a nerd, that guy could design an awesome theatre.

A big-screen television stood in the corner, facing the rest of the room. A white sectional couch that seated five people sat in front of the TV. A speaker system was hooked up to the TV, playing sound from three speakers around the room. In the corner behind the couch, a bar built into the wall housed a mini-fridge and a shelf of snacks and drinks—of the non-alcoholic variety. The bar came with three stools in front of it.

"Carry on, my wayward son! There'll be peace when you are done!"

Pearl smiled as her favorite song started playing from her pocket.

Pearl absolutely loved classic rock, especially Boston and Foreigner. But Kansas' "Carry On, My Wayward Son" was, by far, the best. The way the vocals led the song in, the tenor piercing the group and yet still in harmony. The drums keeping a steady beat, the guitar rocking shrilly throughout the song, the organ barely perceptible in the background, the piano keeping with the melody, the heroic lyrics…Classic rock did not get much better than this.

Pearl pulled out her cell phone.

"Lay your weary head to rest!"

Pearl checked the Caller ID: Sam.

"Don't you cry no more!"

Pearl opened the phone just as the drums started in. "Hello?"

"Hey, Pearl, it's Sam," he answered. "Tell the others that I'm gonna be a little late for movie night. I ran into something here."

"Everything okay?" asked Pearl.

"Yeah, just some museum guy who was interested in the company," Sam told her. "But I'm on my way."

"Okay, I'll tell the gang," said Pearl.

"See you in twenty."

Pearl closed the phone. "That was Sam. He got held up with something about work. He'll be here in twenty minutes."

"Awesome," said Connor. "We'll order pizza while we're waitin'." He grabbed the phone, dialing the delivery place.

"So, what are we watching?" asked Kyle.

"*Back to the Future*," said Chris. "What else would a group of time-travelers watch?"

The girls all laughed at Chris' comment while Connor continued to order their pizzas.

Kyle frowned. "You know, that movie is entirely absurd. Plutonium is highly radioactive. When it's exposed to the air, it expands up to seventy percent of its original volume, which flakes off into the air and accumulates in the bone marrow and liver when inhaled. So, even with their radiation suits, it's not completely ruling out exposure."

"Kyle—" began Katrina.

"Not to mention," Kyle continued, off on his own little roll, "there is no scientific proof that plutonium would be able to generate a reaction related to time travel. Sure, there is a compound of plutonium that is used for nuclear fuel, but it's burned for energy. You wouldn't use it to simply generate a nuclear reaction for electricity."

"Kyle—" tried Mary.

"And where is the dispersing agent?" Kyle went on. "Doc is only using electricity and stainless steel to generate the ability to time travel. He would need a dispersal agent to filter the molecules into the space-time continuum—"

"Kyle!" all six of them cried in unison.

Kyle stopped with a confused look on his face, as though he had just noticed that other people were in the room.

"It's just a movie, Kyle," said Rose. "It's meant to be unrealistic."

"And besides, didn't you base most of your invention on this movie?" Chris pointed out.

"I know, I know," consented Kyle. "It just bugs me, you know. The way a kung fu movie would bother a martial arts expert."

"Well, we'll keep that in mind the next time we pick a movie," said Connor, having finished his order about halfway through Kyle's meltdown.

"And who said this movie is unrealistic?" said Pearl. "It looks pretty believable in my book."

"And you're the girl who thinks *The Matrix* might actually happen someday," Kyle stated.

"Hey, you never know," asserted Pearl. "That could happen. Machines get smarter every day."

"Sure," scoffed Chris. "Pretty soon, they'll be jacking into our brains and using us as batteries."

"Maybe not to that extent," said Pearl. "But they could get smart enough to rebel against us one day."

"And now she's off in *Terminator* land," muttered Kyle.

Pearl looked down at her hands, her face the very picture of frustration. "Sam shares my opinion."

The three guys exchanged amused glances.

"Of course he does," muttered Connor.

"What does that mean?" asked Pearl.

"Nothing," Chris evaded. "Nothing at all."

"Alright, I'm here," said Sam as he entered through the doorway. He plopped down on one of the bar stools. "What'd I miss?"

"Oh, we were just talking about you," Rose told him.

"We were?" asked Sam. "What about?"

"Apparently, nothing at all," said Mary, with a look at Chris.

"You know what?" said Katrina. "I'm starting the movie. Maybe it'll get you guys to shut up."

They all laughed as Katrina began the movie.

~~

Pearl walked into her office. Movie night had been a blast, and it always was.

For some reason, Kyle had told her the night previously to not be in to work before ten. In fact, he had said to just show up whenever she felt like it, as long as she showed up by eleven. He had never done that before, so Pearl was a little confused and on edge.

Pearl noticed an urgent message notice on her computer screen. She clicked on it to read:

MANDATORY MEETING AT ELEVEN O'CLOCK

Pearl's spirit soared; they only had mandatory meetings when they were starting a new project, or someone had just returned from a mission (usually they just had lunch together every day). And since no one had gone on a mission in a month, that meant—

"New project," Pearl said as she smiled. She quickly looked at the clock on her desk: 10:45. "Oh, I made it just in time."

Pearl left her office, heading for their meeting room.

Their agency was a small one-story building. Each of them had their own office room, the majority of which were at the front and middle of the building. Kyle's office was to the left of the front door, Mary's office was in the left front corner of the building, Katrina's office was next to Mary's on the left side of the building, Rose's office was to the right of the front door, Connor's office was in the right front corner of the building, and Chris' office was next to Connor's on the right side of the building.

Katrina had a door leading from her office to the dressing room, which housed the costumes, along the left back side and corner of the building. Chris had a door leading from his office to the library, which housed the records, along the right back side and corner of the building. A meeting room sat at the back of the building next to the dressing room, where they had meetings and ate lunch. A kitchen sat at the back of the building next to the library, where they kept their food and cooked it. In between the meeting room and kitchen was a door that led to the basement, which they called the "Time Lab." It housed the time machine.

In the center of the building sat Sam's and Pearl's offices. Their offices were double the size of the others', Sam being the public relations person and Pearl being the historical consultant. A hallway ran along the back of the building in between the back rooms and their offices. Two restrooms stood across from the kitchen and meeting room.

In front of Sam's and Pearl's offices was a big open area, used for the lobby, project exhibits and waiting area. The exhibits were mostly in front of Pearl's office; the area in front of Sam's office was used as a waiting area for people to meet with him. Along two walls near his office were chairs and couches set up for people to sit in.

Sam scooted up next to her as they walked, his six-foot-whatever frame dwarfing her by about half a head. As he looked down at her, a smile stretched its way across his face, crinkling the skin around his eyes. It gave him a youthful look that practically teemed with childlike innocence.

"Hey, Pearl," said Sam, his green eyes sparkling with anticipation.

Pearl had always loved how vibrant those eyes were; the same way she loved his sandy-blonde hair that was short, yet somewhat shaggy.

"Any idea?" Sam inquired with a smile.

"None," said Pearl, practically skipping. "Wonder what it is."

They entered the meeting room together and sat next to each other around the small table. The meeting room was a good size for the eight of them with a single table in the middle. There was a projector screen on one wall.

Kyle, Katrina, Rose, Mary, Connor and Chris trickled into the room and got seated.

"Hey, guys," said Kyle. "How's everyone's morning been so far?"

"Horrible," muttered Chris with a smile.

"No one asked you, Chris," Kyle told him.

Chris threw out his hands in an indignant gesture while the others laughed.

"Okay, down to business," Kyle said, the smile fading from his lips. "Sam has told me that we've been contacted by a man who is interested in building a museum in Branson for the *Titanic*."

Pearl's heart soared as she and Sam exchanged eager glances. She also shot him a questioning look, wondering why he had not said anything. After all, he was the PR guy.

Sam just gave her a sly glance and a shrug.

"We will be sending someone to April 10, 1912, with a third-class ticket," Kyle went on. "They will cover the majority of the ship, and will stay until the sinking on April 15. And, of course, the person is…"

As Kyle consulted the name in his report, Pearl crossed her fingers under the table.

Please let it be me, she pleaded. *Please…*

"Let me see," mused Kyle. "Where did I put that thing?"

"You are such a tease, Kyle," laughed Mary. "Just get it over with and say it's Pearl already."

They all laughed as Kyle smiled sheepishly.

"Guilty," said Kyle, looking at Pearl. "Pearl, you are chosen to head to *Titanic.*"

She and Sam smiled at each other.

"You will be leaving next Friday and the following Monday will be the meeting to present the information," said Kyle. "Good luck. Now…who wants lunch?"

"No one, Kyle," muttered Connor in a sarcastic tone. "We've been here since eight o'clock. Why would we possibly want food?"

"Well, I was going to pay today, but if you don't want food…" Kyle told him.

Connor straightened up. "Oh, no. You misunderstand me, Kyle. I said we didn't **want** food, but we all **need** food. It has been three or four hours since we ate."

"Uh-huh," said Kyle. "I see."

The others laughed.

27

"What does everyone want?" Kyle asked.

The eight of them began compromising on food choices.

~~

"Can you believe this?" exclaimed Pearl as she and Sam left the building after work. "I mean, me, of all people!"

"Well, how could we not choose you for the *Titanic*?" said Sam. "It's only been your complete obsession since high school." He looked at her. "You have to tell me everything when you get back. I want all the details."

"Looks like I'm not the only one who's excited about this," teased Pearl as they stepped into the ten-car parking lot.

"What can I say?" shrugged Sam. "It's my favorite movie."

"Why didn't you tell me about it before?" Pearl asked.

"What, and ruin the surprise?" Sam laughed. "The best part was that smile on your face."

"You could have at least given me a hint."

"Where's the fun in that?" Sam smiled. He stopped and turned to her as they reached their cars. "You **are** planning on bringing a video camera along, aren't you?"

"You didn't."

"Pearl...I went to World War II. No one wants to see that."

"Good point...Yeah, I will bring a camera."

"So, one week...where do you think you'll start researching?"

"First, I'll look at the ship's schematics so I know my way around the ship. Then I'll make a timeline so I know where to be and when. Then I'll look into my grandfather's adoption."

"Wow..." Sam speculated. "After all these years, you'll finally find the answer to the question that's haunted your family for three generations."

"Yeah," Pearl said.

She could just imagine the look on her mother's and grandfather's faces when she shared the good news.

"Well, let me know how it goes," said Sam as Pearl turned towards her car—a 2001 silver Ford Thunderbird.

"I will," said Pearl. "See you tomorrow."

"See ya," said Sam, making his way towards his own car.

Pearl climbed into her car and began driving to her grandparents' house. They lived in the center of Queens in a charming little neighborhood called Middle Village. As she drove, she turned on her local classic rock radio station, smiling as Def Leppard's "Rock of Ages" began playing.

The drive to the house took twenty minutes, and she parked along the street just outside their house. She walked to the door and knocked, waiting for it to open.

"Pearl!" exclaimed Grandma Kate Livingston as Pearl entered the house. "You made it!"

She hugged Pearl close, Pearl's frame a few inches taller than Kate's.

"You doubted me?" asked Pearl.

Kate smiled, her blue eyes twinkling. "Nonsense. Let me take your coat."

Pearl handed her coat to her grandmother, and Kate hung the coat with the others in the foyer closet.

Pearl headed into the kitchen. "Hey, everyone."

"Hey," came the collective greeting from the people assembled around the table.

The men—excluding Grandpa Sean Livingston—sat at the table while the women bustled about finishing dinner. And wasn't that a typical family dinner: women and the grandparents cooking the meal as the men sat around talking.

"Anything I can help with?" asked Pearl.

"You can help your sister with the pie," her mother, Helen Liberti, told her.

Pearl scooted along the counter until she reached Tru's side. "What do we got?"

"I'm putting the crust into the pan," Tru told her. "You can mix the filling together."

"Will do," said Pearl, turning towards the bowl in front of her. "Ooh, apple! My favorite! Well, second favorite. Nothing can beat chocolate pie."

"You and your pudding, I swear," smiled Tru, tossing her wavy brown hair over her tall, slender shoulder.

"Can you blame me?" said Pearl. "It's the one true dairy product I can eat."

"What, your yogurt doesn't count?"

"Yogurt is lactose-free, and you know it."

Tru laughed. "You're right about that."

"Of course I'm right. I'm older. I'm always right."

Pearl and Tru laughed out loud, drawing the attention of the rest of the family.

"You girls **are** working over there, right?" asked Helen.

"Yes, Mother," the two sisters recited with a snicker.

Pearl had discovered she was lactose intolerant when she was eighteen and working at Dairy Queen, nonetheless. She had just enrolled in college classes the summer right after graduation. She had been having stomach aches regularly and frequently for a few months, but thought it was because of how she was eating: junk food and what not. It was after a certain Anatomy and Physiology class—in which they discussed the digestive tract and disorders pertaining to it—that she decided to test out a theory. She grabbed a cup of ice cream, and…Well, long story short, she discovered the lactose intolerance and had not touched dairy since.

She was grateful that there were still certain dairy foods that she **could** eat. Yogurt is fermented milk, which means it does not have any lactose; the same goes for parmesan cheese and cheddar cheese. The only other dairy product she could eat was pudding. For some reason, it did not affect her—a fact for which she was truly relieved.

Tru looked up at Pearl with her green eyes. "So, Sam ask you out yet?"

Pearl smiled sneakily. "As a matter of fact, he has. We're going to dinner Monday night."

"Ooh, Pearl has a date," Tru sang.

"It is not a date," Pearl insisted. "It's just a dinner between two friends...who happen to maybe like each other."

"Whatever, that is **so** a date," said Tru.

"You're just jealous because the last date you went on was Jarrod Danks at Senior Prom," Pearl teased as she dumped the filling into the crust.

Tru's face turned indignant as she put the top crust on the pie. "I am saving myself for a Texas man."

"Whatever makes you feel better," Pearl stated as she put the pie into the oven.

"Dinner's ready," Kate called.

Helen placed the food on the table as Sean sat at the head of the table.

Pearl's family gathered together for dinner once about every four months: Pearl's mother, grandparents, her mother's brother Andy and family, her father's brother Jake and family, her father's sister Emily and family, and her own baby sister and two brothers. Unfortunately, Pearl's father Tom had died in a car accident shortly after Tru was born.

The patriarch of the family—Sean Livingston—had been born with red hair, which had now turned white in his old age. He also had green eyes, which he had passed on to his and his wife Kate's daughter Helen.

Helen had passed on her slender frame and medium height to Pearl. Helen also had blonde hair and green eyes. Helen had married Tom Liberti, who had a tall stature with light brown hair and blue eyes.

Helen had passed on her eyes to every one of her children, so Pearl and her three siblings all had green eyes.

The eldest, John, got his red hair from Helen's side of the family, but had inherited his tall stature from Tom. He was the protector of the siblings, always watching over his brothers and sisters.

The youngest boy Leo got his blonde hair from Helen, along with his height. He was the most level-headed of the bunch.

The youngest of the family, Tru, got her brown hair and stature from Tom. She also got her stubborn will from Tom.

Pearl, being the second child, played the peace-keeper of the family. She always had to separate Leo and Tru from their stupid fights. Sure, Leo was the level-headed one, but he and Tru were also the youngest of the family. Of course, they fought all the time—more when they were kids than when they grew up.

As soon as they said grace, they dug in. Pearl took a breath and addressed the group.

"I have an announcement to make," Pearl said.

Everyone looked up and paused.

"I have been chosen for a project at work to go back to the *Titanic*," Pearl announced with a smile.

The family started congratulating her.

"That's wonderful!" Aunt Emily told her.

"What are the odds?" said Uncle Andy.

Pearl looked specifically at her grandfather. "I'll finally be able to find out who your parents were."

Everyone grew silent.

"I hope so," Sean answered her.

"When do you leave?" asked Uncle Jake.

"Next Friday," Pearl answered.

"We should all get together that Sunday for dinner," Kate told them. "Pearl can share her discoveries."

"And video," Pearl added.

"Video?" asked Helen.

"Yes, I'm taking a camera with me, so everyone can see it all," said Pearl.

Tru smiled. "Well, that ought to be interesting."

~~

Pearl walked into the library at work and started searching the Schematics Archives.

"Q...S...T," Pearl muttered as she walked down the aisle. "*Titanic...Titanic...Titanic...*"

"Need help?" asked Chris.

Pearl turned to see him standing behind her.

"You hid the *Titanic* stuff, didn't you?" she said, a hand on her hip.

Chris laughed. "It's right over here."

He led her down the aisle to a small section of the shelves labeled "*Titanic.*"

Pearl smiled. "Thanks."

"Just let me know if you get lost again," Chris told her as he headed back to his desk.

Pearl laughed. "Will do."

Pearl pulled the rolled-up blueprints from the shelf and headed for the history books. When she made it to a table to begin research, she had many books, such as <u>Titanic: A History</u>, <u>A Night to Remember</u>, and <u>An Illustrated History of the Ship of Dreams</u>.

Pearl began pouring over the schematics, cross-referencing one blueprint with another. She then poured through the books, connecting one event to another. By the end of her session, she had pulled together a rough timeline of events.

Her phone started vibrating, and she looked at the screen:

FITTING MONDAY – 10 AM

Pearl put a reminder on her phone and gathered her things together.

Ah, the dreaded costume fitting, she thought.

Every agent had to go to a fitting for their period clothes, and it was always a hassle—almost always a hassle.

Pearl walked out to her car and drove home, hoping for a restful weekend.

3

Teamwork

Pearl walked into the dressing room to find the team of costume designers—which, in truth, consisted solely of Katrina and Mary—and her best friend there.

"Hey!" said Sam. He came and hugged Pearl. "So, four days, huh?"

Sam pulled away and took a good look at her. Pearl's eyes were bloodshot, and her face looked clammy.

"Are you okay?" Sam asked. "You look a little pale."

"I had that dream again," Pearl told him in an undertone.

Sam looked around to make sure the other two girls were not listening and whispered, "You mean the one where you're on the stern of the *Titanic* as it sinks?"

"Yeah," said Pearl as her breathing became shallow.

Sam placed his hands on her arms and rubbed them, consoling her. "Hey, don't worry about it; you're not gonna die. You have an advantage: you know what's coming. Secondly, you have the pendant. You can press it at any time. You don't have to become one of the casualties."

Pearl exhaled. "Casualties...How can something so horrible sound so cavalier?"

Sam gave a small smile. "Sorry. Side-effect of war: you know, hardening of emotions. It happens to most World War II veterans. I didn't mean any disrespect."

Pearl shook her head. "It's not that I'm afraid of dying; I know it won't get that far. It's just...being there as those people die...feeling their fear...knowing I can't do anything to save them. It's just going to be hard."

Sam pulled her into a hug and held her. "Don't worry. Everything will be all right. I'll be there every step of the way."

Pearl frowned in confusion. "You will?"

Sam shrugged. "Well...in spirit."

Pearl gave a small laugh as they broke apart.

"Ah, Pearl," Katrina said as she and Mary approached. "Congratulations on the *Titanic* project. Now, I have some outfits for you to try on here. Not only do we have third-class dress, but we have your first-class apparel as well."

They began walking towards the podium in front of the mirrors as Pearl tried to wrap her mind around what she had just heard.

"Wait...first **and** third-class?" Pearl inquired. "Why two?"

"It'll all be explained at tomorrow's briefing," Mary told her. "Right now, we just focus on the clothes."

"I'll see you later, Pearl," Sam said as he turned to leave.

"Okay," Pearl told him.

Katrina led her to a changing room filled with dresses. Half of the ensembles were classy and flamboyant, and the other half were simple and traditional.

"Wow, you guys did a great job," Pearl congratulated them. "I see you've made excellent use of those period clothing pictures I gave you."

"Hey, it's our job," said Mary. "You supply us with the information, and we make the miracles happen."

"How long did you guys work on these?" asked Pearl.

"Longer than any other project," muttered Mary.

Pearl chuckled. "I can believe that."

"We worked all weekend," Katrina told her.

"Well, this is great," Pearl repeated.

"Alright, have fun," said Katrina as they left Pearl to change.

The first outfit Pearl tried on was a third-class dress: brown cotton with a white shawl. There were two more of the same fashion, and she switched over to first-class.

As it turned out, there were a fair few more first-class dresses than third. Pearl figured it was because first-class women changed dresses twice a day, necessitating the more extensive wardrobe.

The last outfit to try on was a first-class dress. She came out of the dressing room and climbed onto the podium.

"I haven't gotten this dressed up since Prom," Pearl laughed.

The dress she had on at the moment was a stunning shade of scarlet with a white lace covering over the red silk. The sleeves went down to Pearl's elbows, and they were white lace. The dress came with a small train, and an ornate, pearl headpiece. Her hair was done up in a bun, and the pearl strings were looped all over her hair. She was also wearing authentic black shoes, white gloves, a pearl necklace, and bracelets and rings.

As Pearl was admiring herself in the mirror, she saw Sam enter behind her.

"Good news, Pearl," Sam announced as he looked at his PDA. "I've talked with Chris, and he says we can…"

Sam had just looked up at Pearl and took sight of her in the first-class dress. He became speechless as he gazed at Pearl.

"Wow…" he muttered.

Pearl turned towards him and smiled at his stammering.

"You look…breathtaking…" breathed Sam.

Pearl beamed at him. "Thank you. What do you think? Can I pass as a Kate Winslet?"

Sam stepped closer. "Kate Winslet's got nothing on you."

Pearl smiled, feeling a blush appear on her face. "What did Chris say?"

Sam frowned, drawn out of the earlier conversation. "What?"

"When you came in, you said that Chris said we could…" Pearl hinted.

Sam seemed to startle a little as he caught up with Pearl. "Oh, right!"

Mary and Katrina exchanged an amused smile at the way Sam and Pearl were acting.

"Uh, he said we could move the briefing to Thursday so you have tomorrow and Wednesday to finish your research," Sam told Pearl.

"Great," smiled Pearl. She began to turn around to face the mirrors, but then remembered something. "Oh, I made an appointment for tomorrow with the agency that handled my grandfather's adoption. They arranged a meeting with a woman who was actually there when my grandfather was dropped off."

"Really?" Sam wondered. "How old is she?"

"One hundred and three last month," Pearl informed him as she headed back to the dressing room.

"And she's **working** at the agency?" asked Sam.

"Yep," Pearl told him.

Sam's eyebrows rose. "Wow."

"She says she has some very valuable information for me," said Pearl.

"Great," Sam said. "I'm glad for you. Is this it for you? You're free for dinner?"

"Yeah, just give me a minute. I'm almost done."

Pearl retreated to the changing room, attempting to undo her dress and jewelry. She huffed in exasperation after three failed attempts.

"Katrina!" Pearl called. "I need a little help in here!"

Katrina eased the curtain open enough to enter the changing room, closing the curtain again. "It's tough, isn't it? The women who usually wore these clothes had a maid to help them into and out of it. You'll get the hang of it in time."

Katrina eased the headpiece off of Pearl's head, trying to refrain from snagging the pearls in her hair. Pearl removed her gloves as Katrina set the pearls on the table in the room. Once all the jewelry was removed, Pearl turned to face the wall so Katrina could get at the buttons on the back of the dress.

"Here, step over here," said Katrina. She ushered Pearl over towards the mirror. "Here, watch while I unbutton it."

Pearl gazed over her shoulder into the mirror and watched as Katrina pulled the small buttons through the holes. She then pulled the silk strings through the loops of the corset, untying it. When it was loose enough, Pearl eased it down her torso and stepped out of it.

"Ugh, finally," Pearl muttered, feeling much more comfortable in her tankini and briefs. "Thanks."

"No problem," said Katrina, laying the dress carefully with the others. "Now, go get your man."

Pearl whipped her head over to Katrina, eyes wide and a smile breaking over her face. "Katrina!"

"What?" said Katrina, a smile also on her face. "It's obvious he likes you."

"But you don't just go blurting that out," Pearl told her in a hushed voice. "He's right outside. What if he heard you?"

"Oh, come on," Katrina laughed. "It's fine."

Pearl pulled her jeans on and slid her shirt over her head. "You know, I thought when I told you I had feelings for Sam that I was telling the reliable one of the team. I don't need you blurting my secret out everywhere."

41

"Oh, I'm **not** the reliable one," said Katrina, making her way towards the curtain. "Okay. I'll just go tell Sam, then."

Pearl darted for her friend, pulling her away from the curtain. "You will not!"

Katrina collapsed into Pearl's arms as the two of them laughed. Pearl fixed her hair in the mirror and gave Katrina a look as she headed for the curtain.

"Go get him, girl," said Katrina, slapping her friend on the shoulder as she walked past her.

Pearl smiled as she made her way into the main room, where Sam stood by the window. He turned towards Pearl, smiling as she walked towards him.

"Shall we?" said Pearl, taking Sam by the elbow and heading for the door.

Sam led her to his car, a cherry red 1972 Dodge Challenger. The two of them absolutely loved classic cars, especially the Chevys and the Dodges.

Pearl's dream car of choice—if she ever found one for a low enough amount and in good condition—was a royal blue 1967 Chevy Impala. Everyone always said that the Impala was not in even when it was in. Pearl supposed that was the reason why she liked it so much. It was rare that you saw one of the old Impalas on the road. It was more of a muscle car than a classic, and it looked just beautiful tearing down the road.

Pearl climbed into the passenger's seat of the Challenger as Sam climbed into the other side, starting up the engine. It purred to life, humming through the metal frame. Pearl smiled as Sam pulled out of the parking space and headed into traffic. Within fifteen wonderful minutes of riding in the classic, Sam pulled into the restaurant where they had their reservation.

They entered the restaurant, being seated by the hostess.

"This place is nice," Pearl commented. "Thank you."

"You're welcome," Sam told her, picking up his menu.

The two of them read through the options before a dark-haired man in black pants, white shirt, black vest and black tie came up to the table. He pulled out a pad of paper as he stood next to the table.

"How may I help you?" asked the waiter, putting a pen to his pad of paper.

"Yes, we'd like two glasses of your finest wine, please," Sam told the waiter. "And I'll have the shrimp scampi."

"And I'll have the fettuccini pasta with the chicken sauce," Pearl told the waiter.

The waiter stalked off to place their order.

"So, how're you feeling?" Sam inquired.

Pearl looked up at him and frowned in confusion.

"What do you mean?" she asked him.

"Well, I mean…with the big day only four days away…You must be a little nervous."

"Not until you brought it up."

Sam stammered a little. "I-I didn't mean to—"

"I'm kidding, Sam," Pearl teased.

The waiter walked over to the table, pouring wine into their glasses.

"It's weird," Pearl confessed. "I should be anxious and nervous, but I'm...not."

"Probably because you're so excited," said Sam. "This is your dream come true."

As the waiter walked away, Sam picked up his wine glass.

"Congratulations...to the future," he toasted.

"You mean the past?" Pearl taunted, smiling at him as she raised her own glass.

Sam smiled at her as they lightly clinked their glasses together. They both sipped their wine as they held each other's gaze for several moments. Something silently passed between the two of them, and everything seemed to click into place.

As Pearl began to realize that there was something special between them, Sam reached forward tentatively and grasped her hand. Pearl responded by placing her other hand over his. They enjoyed the moment as they stared into each other's eyes.

~~

Pearl pushed open the door to the adoption agency, Charion United. It was a very nice facility and well-respected. To the right was a small office that looked fairly busy. Ahead and to the left was a dormitory hall full of rooms for the children. A sign hung on the wall that detailed which children went where. It read:

1st floor: newborns

2nd floor: 1-3 year olds

3rd floor: 4-7 year olds

4th floor: 8-12 year olds
5th floor: 13 plus

Pearl ventured down the hall to explore the agency. Halfway down the hall were two wings, one on each side. The right was labeled "boys," and the left labeled "girls."

"Miss Liberti?" came a frail voice from the office behind her.

Pearl spun to face an elderly woman who was in a wheelchair. The woman pushing her was very young, probably in her twenties.

"Hi, I'm Pearl Liberti," Pearl greeted as she walked over and shook the elderly woman's hand. "Thanks for meeting with me, Mrs. Vandez."

"It's my pleasure," Elizabeth Vandez told her. She began staring at Pearl as if appreciating her. "Remarkable…"

"What's remarkable?"

"You look just like…someone," Elizabeth told her. She frowned as she tried to remember. "I've seen her before." She looked back up at Pearl. "I swear I've seen you before."

"Maybe it'll come to you later," suggested Pearl.

"Yes, maybe," said Elizabeth.

Pearl smiled and took the wheelchair from the young woman.

"My office is just up here," Elizabeth informed her.

Pearl began pushing the chair in that direction. "So, were you really here when my grandfather was adopted, Mrs. Vandez?"

"Please, call me Lizzy," she replied.

"Okay, Lizzy."

"Yes, I was here. I was ten years old that night in 1912. I was one of the orphans, and I grew up to work here."

45

They entered her office, and Pearl sat down opposite Lizzy.

"And I know what you must be thinking," said Lizzy. "Why is an old woman like me still working here?"

The two of them laughed.

"I couldn't retire," Lizzy explained. "I just love this place so much." She frowned. "What were we talking about earlier?"

"The night my grandfather was dropped off," Pearl reminded her, beginning to get doubtful about her memory skills.

"Ah, yes," Lizzy smiled. "Not to worry, dearie. I may forget things occasionally, but my memory is still as fresh as it ever was. I remember that night like it was yesterday. It was April 18…the very night the *Carpathia* docked in New York. A young lady came in; she couldn't have been more than eighteen years old. She told us that she had found the baby in a suitcase floating next to the bodies."

Pearl froze at that statement, shocked that she was hearing this. It could not possibly be real, could it?

"After a lifeboat came back for survivors, a woman was fished out of the water with a suitcase. There was a baby inside, but the woman said it wasn't hers. The young lady who came to the orphanage couldn't stand to watch him suffer. She took it upon herself to watch over the boy until she found the parents, but they were never found. She said we should find a suitable family." Elizabeth's face suddenly brightened in recognition. "That's where I remember you from."

"What?" asked Pearl.

"Who you remind me of," Elizabeth elaborated. "There was a woman who came in with the young lady with the baby. It was the same woman who had brought the suitcase to the lady's boat. You have her eyes. And that beautiful face with her ruby red hair…she was an angel."

"Do you remember their names?" asked Pearl as the old legend came back into her mind.

"Uh…not both of them, but I believe I know the name of the lady who brought the baby in."

Elizabeth pulled out a paper from her file, searching for the name.

Is it Cecily Miles? Pearl thought, anxious. *If it's Cecily Miles, then my great grandparents are—*

"Ah, yes. Her name was Cecily Miles."

4

Family Secrets

Pearl hurried into the agency, trying to keep herself calm. What would Sam say when he heard this? This was the biggest scoop of her entire life. How could she not have seen it before? She had heard the story so many times. How did she not put the pieces together?

All this rattled through her head as she raced through the empty waiting room for Sam's office. She made it to the door and knocked.

"Come in!" came a pleasant voice.

Pearl opened the door to see Sam hunched over a keyboard. She came in and shut the door. She was clutching the envelope Elizabeth had given her.

Sam looked up at her from his desk. "Hey, how'd the appointment go?"

"Oh, you know…same old, same old." Pearl looked at him and blurted, "I found my grandfather's real parents."

Sam stopped and faced her. "Really? Who? John Jacob Astor? Molly Brown? Isidor and Ida Straus?"

Sam had been just randomly spouting names associated with the *Titanic*. Even though he was a real fan of the story, he did not know as many facts about it as Pearl did…and he knew it.

Pearl hesitated. "Lachlan and Constance Dunleavy."

For a moment, Sam was silent, as though unsure if Pearl was joking or not. After a long pause, he laughed hesitantly.

"Pearl, the story of Lachlan and Constance Dunleavy is just a myth. They're fictional."

"They existed," Pearl said as she hastily pulled out the paper and handed it to him. "Look." She pointed at the name of the person who found her grandfather. "That's the woman who brought my grandfather in to the adoption agency."

"Pearl, that could be any twenty-year-old named Cecily Miles," Sam tried to convince her.

"A twenty-year-old who just happens to have the legendary suitcase with her?" said Pearl.

Sam stared in confusion.

Pearl grabbed a magnifier from the edge of the desk. "Look at the bag in the background."

Sam took the magnifier and peered into the photograph.

A black and brown leather-lined suitcase sat behind the young woman. A big brass lock adorned the front, held in place by a leather clasp. Two straps ran over the top of the lid, and leather handles were fastened on the sides of the suitcase. Underneath the handles, Sam could just barely make out the initials at the bottom of the suitcase: Z.F.A.[1]

Sam then gazed up at Pearl, perplexed. "How?"

"Well, it's not that big of a stretch to think that it could really have happened. I mean, people think it was just a myth, but ninety-percent of the time, myths are based on fact. The story goes that Lachlan and Constance both set sail on the *Titanic* to escape the persecution of Irish Catholics. They both went down with the ship, but not before placing their newborn son into an empty suitcase that was floating nearby; a suitcase with the initials Z.F.A. on it.

"When a woman was brought into a lifeboat, they also pulled the suitcase in with a baby inside. Cecily Miles took the baby and the suitcase and brought them onboard the *Carpathia*. Now, that very suitcase is on display in a *Titanic* exhibit in New York. The only things found inside were a small orange purse, a bracelet and a woman's blue dress jacket. And they say this is the very suitcase they found the baby in…my grandfather."

"Oh, gosh…The whole story is true…and you're gonna be right in the middle of it. How does that feel?"

"Amazing…and terrifying."

"Remember: you can't interfere with their lives, no matter how much you may want to. Anything you change could have serious repercussions on future events."

"Right." Pearl paused. "Pearl Dunleavy…I like the sound of that."

---

[1] This suitcase is the exact same one displayed in the *Titanic* museum in Branson, Missouri.

"Actually, your last name wouldn't be Dunleavy because that would be your mother's maiden name."

"You just ruin everyone's fun, don't you?"

Sam smiled as he turned back to the computer.

Pearl opened her mouth to speak, but faltered as her heart started to quicken its pace. She took a deep breath and tried again.

"Would you like to come over and watch the movie tonight?" Pearl forced out despite her pumping adrenaline.

Sam turned and looked at her. He smiled as Pearl waited for his answer.

"I'd love to," Sam answered. He looked at his watch, a smile suddenly working its way onto his face. "Come on, it's lunch time."

Sam stood up and latched his hand onto Pearl's, a smirk forming among his smile.

"Oh, no," said Pearl. "I don't like that look on your face. It always means trouble."

"Don't know what you're talking about," smiled Sam, avoiding her eyes and drawing her close. "It's lunch. What could possibly happen?"

"Knowing you, anything," said Pearl, following him towards the office meeting room.

Sam opened the door, stepping aside. Pearl found four pizza boxes on the table, the six others standing in the room.

"Surprise!" cheered Katrina, a big smile on her face.

"We felt bad for not celebrating sooner," explained Mary.

"Celebrating what?" asked Pearl.

"Landin' a *Titanic* project," said Connor with his Texan accent. "We all know how much ya love that story."

Pearl smiled sheepishly. Anytime she read a new book about the *Titanic*, she had not wasted any time in telling everyone all the new trivia she had learned. She tended to talk someone's ear off if they got her started on something.

"And that's not all," said Rose.

Rose stepped away from the counter, turning around. An ice cream cake lay in her arms. Pearl gave her an unsure look.

"Don't worry; it's frozen yogurt," Rose reassured her.

"You guys..." said Pearl, taken aback.

"I know," said Chris. "We're the best, huh?"

"Of course, you do realize that since we threw this party, we now have no money for the actual trip," said Rose.

Pearl looked up at her, hand on her hip. "Very funny."

They all laughed as they served up pizza and cake. All eight of them sat at the round table in the middle of the room. Halfway through their celebrations, Kyle looked up at Pearl.

"You find out anything?" he asked.

The others froze, staring at Pearl. Everyone knew what he was referring to.

"Actually, I have," Pearl started, exchanging a sly glance with Sam. "My great grandparents were—wait for it—Lachlan and Constance Dunleavy."

"No way!" said Rose. "That's awesome!"

"Ya mean to tell me that yur grandfather was the baby in the suitcase at that museum?" asked Connor.

"Yep," said Pearl. "Now I just have to find out who that woman is."

"What woman?" asked Chris.

"The woman that brought the suitcase to Cecily's boat," said Pearl. "She never had a name in the legend. I wonder who she was."

"Well, you'll find out in a week," said Kyle. "Just try not to change history."

"I can't guarantee anything," Pearl told him with a serious face.

Kyle gave her a pointed, wide-eyed look that had everyone laughing. He pointed his spoon at her. "You better change your answer, girl."

Pearl laughed as she got lost in her vanilla frozen yogurt.

~~

Pearl took out a bag of popcorn and a bowl. She placed the popcorn in the microwave and started it up. She then rushed through the dining room and into the living room to straighten the couch out. She turned the television on and put the DVD in the player. She turned the VCR off and put the remote on the coffee table.

The doorbell rang, and Pearl hurried through the archway and down the hallway to the foyer. She opened the front door to find Sam standing on the porch with a nervous smile on his face. He was wearing jeans and a light blue, long-sleeve, button-down shirt; just perfect for the occasion. He was carrying a single long-stemmed rose in his hand.

"What do you think?" Sam asked as he smirked. "Too formal?"

"No…it's just right," Pearl replied.

Sam offered her the rose as he came in. Pearl accepted it and smelled the bud. She closed the door as Sam headed to the living room.

Pearl headed down the hallway on the right of the staircase and headed for the archway to the kitchen. Pearl set the rose on the counter and retrieved the popcorn out of the microwave and dumped it into the bowl. When she returned to the living room with a bowl of popcorn in one hand and the rose in the other, Sam had already sat down with the remote.

Pearl sat down next to Sam as he turned the VCR on, placing the rose on the coffee table and the popcorn on her lap for him to reach. Pearl folded her legs up next to her on the couch while Sam placed a blanket over the both of them.

The main menu popped onto the screen, filling the room with the rising music. Sam pressed play and put an arm around Pearl. She leaned into him as the sepia-toned 1912 clips of the *Titanic*'s departure from Southampton played to the soft Irish music.

~~

"She was such a beautiful ship; she was so lovely…That's how we ought to remember her."[2]

As Eva Hart concluded, the screen switched to Jack and Fabrizio on the bow as the music climaxed and the credits sprang up.

---

2 From Fox's "Breaking New Ground."

Sam pressed the stop button and looked down at Pearl.

After the movie was over, they had put on the Fox Special: Breaking New Ground that came with the DVD. Pearl had fallen asleep half an hour into it. Now, Pearl's head was planted against Sam's leg on a pillow.

Sam placed an arm across his lap and stroked the hair out of her face. He turned the television off and carefully navigated from under Pearl without waking her. He placed one arm under her legs and one under her shoulders. As gently as he could, he picked her up in his arms.

Sam walked towards the stairs and headed up to the second floor. He turned left down the hallway at the top of the stairs, heading to the master bedroom. Without turning on the lights, he placed Pearl onto the bed, wrapping the covers around her. Pearl shifted in her sleep, finding a more comfortable position. Her eyes remained closed, deep in dreaming. Sam tucked the blankets under her chin and placed a hand on her forehead.

"You will always be my beautiful pearl," Sam whispered.

He then walked to the doorway taking one last look before shutting the door quietly.

5

Unbelievable Journey

"Pearl! Pearl!"

Pearl jolted awake to find Sam sitting on her desk. She looked at the clock: 10:15. She had only been asleep for five minutes.

Pearl smiled, touching her hand to her chin. "You wouldn't let me walk out of here with drool on my face, would you?"

Sam laughed. "Neither of us got much sleep last night, did we?"

"What can I say? The movie's over three hours long."

"How's the research coming?" Sam asked, changing tracks.

"Well, I've been able to modify my timeline and to-do list to include the movie's events. Here's the plan: I have a first-class dinner on the tenth, report to the Boat Deck for full speed ahead on the eleventh, have a third-class dinner that night, first-class dinner on the twelfth, attend a third-class party on the thirteenth, attend mass on Sunday morning, take the tour with Thomas Andrews, watch *Titanic*'s last sunset, watch the collision, and randomly go throughout the ship for the sinking."

"Looks like you've got it all figured out."

"Pretty much. I better get moving. I've got to drive across town and meet with a member of the *Titanic* Historical Society."

"Well, I'll let you get back to it."

Sam got up and exited the office.

Pearl gathered up all of her research and stuffed it into her briefcase. She then made her way to the parking lot, climbing into her Thunderbird. The ride to the society took only about fifteen minutes. Pearl exited her car and walked to the front door.

Hanna Maria Wetter was waiting in the lobby for her, and she held her hand out.

"Pearl Liberti," she said. "I'm Hanna Wetter. Welcome to the *Titanic* Historical Society."

"Thanks for meeting with me," Pearl told her as they walked up towards her office.

"It's my pleasure," Hanna told her. "The BHCA is well-respected; it's an honor to have you here."

When they reached her office, they sat down on the couch in the corner.

"I just have a few questions to straighten out," Pearl began as she pulled her research out. "Mostly about events onboard the ship."

"Anything you need," Hanna said as she smiled.

~~

Pearl put down her fork as her family continued their conversation.

It was only the immediate family: Pearl and her siblings, their mother and their grandparents. Pearl's older brother John sat to her right. Her younger brother Leo sat in front of her across the table next to their mother Helen. The baby of the family, her sister Tru, sat on Pearl's left. Kate and Sean sat at either end of the table.

"Pearl," Sean said.

Pearl looked up at her grandfather.

"Have you found anything out about my parents?" asked Sean.

The table fell silent as Pearl hesitated.

"Actually, I have," Pearl told them. "This is going to be hard to believe, but it's true...Grandpa's parents...were Lachlan and Constance Dunleavy. The couple that placed their infant son in a suitcase that Cecily Miles found."

Everyone was speechless. Pearl pulled out the photograph of Cecily with baby Sean in her arms. She showed it to everyone.

"Sean Dunleavy," said her grandfather, smiling fondly. He looked up at her. "They were real?"

"Absolutely," Pearl responded. "I just want to find out who the mystery woman that brought the suitcase to the lifeboat was. The strange thing is that the woman I talked to at the orphanage said I looked like the woman."

"Maybe it was Constance," Tru speculated. "Maybe she didn't die."

"But then why would she give her son away?" said Pearl. "That doesn't make any sense."

"Well, maybe…" began John, glancing cautiously at Sean, "maybe after losing Lachlan, she didn't want to be reminded of him." He looked apologetically at his grandfather. "No offense."

"None taken," Sean shrugged off the comment.

"No," said Pearl. "I mean, we've never met her, but I can't believe she would just do that to her own son."

"Well, that's one thing you're gonna have to find out for yourself," said Leo.

"Looks like," said Pearl.

~~

Pearl closed her front door as she tossed the keys onto the table right next to her. She bolted the door and set the alarm, feeling safe. She kicked off her shoes and made her way to her room.

Once she had changed into more comfortable clothes, she curled up on the couch in the living room and began flipping through the channels. The channel that popped onto the screen when the television turned on was an infomercial.

"Take advantage of this limited time offer," said the saleswoman. *"You can have the pendant and the necklace for only—"*

Pearl flipped to the next channel, finding a news report.

"Authorities have identified the suspect as Richard Carson," announced the anchorman. *"He is believed to be—"*

Pearl flipped to the next channel, recognizing a rerun of a television episode.

"Well, far be it from me to violate the chain of command," ex-Manticore soldier Alec quipped in a sarcastic tone with a cocky smile.

Pearl paused in her channel flipping. *Dark Angel* used to be one of her favorite television shows. She just had to watch for a moment. Jensen Ackles had a perfect comedic timing. She watched as Jensen's character Alec dished out more jokes and taunts.

Pearl huffed out a small chuckle, flipping through a couple more channels. She finally stopped on the History Channel, which was showing *Ghosts of the Abyss*.

"Imagine that," Pearl muttered to herself. "They just happen to be showing James Cameron's documentary about the *Titanic*."

As she laughed at the irony, her eyes fell on the rose that was still on the coffee table. She reached over and picked it up, bringing it to her nose and inhaling. It was the most beautiful smell she had ever experienced.

Pearl's thoughts drifted to Sam and their unofficial date last night. Sure, he was cute, but was there something there? And how could she be sure he felt the same way?

Pearl pondered this as she got lost in the History Channel.

~~

Pearl entered the meeting room and sat at one side of the table. Kyle and Chris were on the other side.

"Thanks for coming, Pearl," Kyle said as Pearl opened her folder. "First off, I wanted to say congratulations. I know you've been waiting for this for a long time."

"Thank you," Pearl replied politely.

"Now, down to business," Kyle began.

Pearl checked her schedule and research as he spoke.

"You will be covering the first and third-class areas, including the Palm Court Café, first-class suites and corridors, upper decks and Boat Deck, the bridge, steerage common room and gymnasium. You will be on deck for launching from Southampton and the iceberg collision.

"There are several controversies we would like to settle: the fate of Captain Smith, whether or not the band played 'Nearer, My God, to Thee' as their final song, whether the conversation between Ismay and Smith about the ship's speed took place, whether passengers were shot, and the fate of First Officer Murdoch.

"Also, the forward grand staircase is missing in the wreck. We would like you to find out what happened to it during the sinking. Any questions?"

"No," answered Pearl.

"Well, then..." Kyle said as they all stood up. "Good luck, Pearl. You can use the rest of the day for preparation. We will see you in the Time Lab at eleven o'clock tomorrow morning." He turned to Chris. "Now that we got business out of the way..."

Chris smiled. "Pizza?"

Kyle nodded. "Pizza." He looked at Pearl. "Care to join us?"

"Maybe another time," Pearl laughed.

"Suit yourself," said Chris as he and Kyle left the room.

Pearl followed the two of them out of the room, heading down the hall ahead of her. Thoughts began to creep into her mind about the mission. What if she died? It was highly unlikely, but what if...

If this was her last day on earth, who would she want to spend it with?

A smile crept its way onto her face as she thought about her answer.

Pearl made her way around the corner to the left at the end of the hall, opening the door to the office in front of her.

"Hey," Pearl greeted the occupant. "Got a minute?"

~~

"I'm glad you decided to play hooky with me," Pearl told Sam as they sat in the park.

"No problem," Sam replied.

"I just...I was thinking of who I'd want to spend my last day on earth with, and—" began Pearl.

"And I was the one who popped into your head?"

"Yeah," Pearl said as she looked up at the majestic oak trees.

A pond shimmered in the sunlight in front of them, the brilliant rays reflecting onto the trees, creating small pinpoints of light and dancing over everything. A bridge towered over the water, linking the two sides of the pond. The turtles swam in small circles, poking their heads up for air every once in a while and creating ripples on the pond's surface.

The trees stretched towards the sky, the green, needled branches fashioning a canopy over the bench where the two of them sat. Brown pine needles littered the stone-paved walkway, producing the illusion of naturalness among the manmade structure.

A soft breeze blew through the park, offering a pleasant change of pace from the sweltering heat of July that they had been experiencing the past month. Swallows flew above the trees around them, creating soft streams of song in the afternoon air.

Pearl sighed. "It's all so beautiful. I can't imagine never seeing this again."

"Hey…" Sam told her as he placed his hands on her shoulders. "You will see these trees again someday. You're gonna make it back."

"I hope you're right," Pearl whispered as a tear fell down her cheek.

"I don't have to hope; I know. We will see each other again." He pulled her into his arms and gently held her. "It'll be okay."

"I know it will," Pearl said as she held onto him. "I'll have you to guide me."

"You bet you will," said Sam. He pulled away from Pearl and stood, holding his arm out. "Would you like an escort home?"

Pearl smiled as she stood and hooked her arm through his. "I would love one."

Pearl figured that they could walk since this was the park three blocks from her house. She had decided to leave her car at work since Sam had offered to give her a ride tomorrow.

As Sam walked her up the steps to her door, she gave him a smile.

"See you tomorrow morning, then," Pearl told him.

"Yeah…tomorrow," Sam smiled. "Good night."

"Good night," Pearl said, entering her house for what she hoped would not be the final time.

~~

Pearl woke up at nine on Friday. The other seven had already arrived at the BHCA to set up the machine and make arrangements for the operation. Pearl had been allowed to sleep in to rest up for the day.

Pearl crawled out of bed and got dressed. After dinner last night, she had gone to bed thinking about Sam. It's amazing how you can know someone your entire life and your feelings suddenly change.

As she prepared to leave her house, she left a note for Sam on the table next to the door. If she did not come home, she had to let Sam know how she felt.

Pearl heard a car horn bleep from outside and knew Sam had arrived. She locked the door and headed for his car.

"Hey," greeted Pearl as she jumped into his car.

"Sleep well?" Sam asked, pulling away from her house.

"Well enough," Pearl told him, staring through the windshield.

Pearl's mind wandered back to her research as Sam drove them to work. She went over everything she was supposed to do in the next week of her life. Before she knew it, they had reached the building.

Pearl walked through the halls towards the time lab, wringing her hands in front of her in anticipation as Sam followed her. Reaching the end of the hall, she turned right and headed for the door in between the kitchen and meeting room, which read "Authorized

Personnel Only." She took a deep breath and opened the door, heading down the stairs towards the basement. The stairs ended in a large observation room, where her family stood waiting for her.

As she smiled at her family, Mary came over and escorted her into a small dressing room. The wardrobe change seemed to drag on until she was finally done.

Pearl came out of the dressing room in a green cotton dress with a plaid shawl tied around her shoulders. The waiting room was filled with Pearl's family and friends. The day had finally come; Pearl was about to travel through time.

Pearl said goodbye to each member of her family. There were hugs and a few tears. Kyle came over and handed Pearl her pendant.

"Good luck, Pearl," he told her. "Here is your ticket and camera." He handed her the ticket and the spectacles containing a hidden camera. "We'll bring your luggage in later. Don't lose any of it."

"I won't," Pearl assured him.

In the lab behind them, the lights sprang into existence. Illuminated in the center was the time machine. It was a giant moving platform that would ascend into a glass dome. Under the platform sat a tank of water with a diamond underneath. The diamond would focus on a moving timeline on the floor under the tank. Inside the glass dome, electricity dischargers connected to gold, copper and stainless steel conducting wires, which ran around the glass dome into the water tank.

Pearl took a deep breath and waved goodbye to her family. She turned and looked at Sam. He walked over and hugged her.

"I'll be with you," Sam whispered. "Just tell yourself that whenever it feels like all is lost."

He let her go and put his hand in his pocket. Pearl looked down as he pulled his hand out, clutching a necklace. Pearl smiled, staring in shock. The necklace he held in his hand was a silver, heart-shaped locket with a blue sapphire in it.

"Sam..." Pearl whispered, unable to voice her appreciation.

"Think of it as a reminder of me," Sam told her as he clasped it around her neck. "It'll help."

"Really?"

"It helped me," Sam admitted. "Whenever times got tough, I, uh...I thought of you."

Pearl smiled and hugged him.

"Pearl," Kyle urged, "it's time."

Pearl unfolded herself from Sam's embrace and held his hands for a moment.

"Oh," Pearl remembered suddenly. "I almost forgot."

She headed for the pile of clothes she had left in the changing room. Digging a key out of her pocket, she walked back to Sam, holding it up.

"For later," said Pearl, handing it to him.

Understanding, Sam pocketed the key.

Pearl waved goodbye to everyone as she entered the lab. They escorted her over to the machine, and she placed herself in the middle of the platform.

Chris, Katrina and Mary carried in three old-fashioned luggage bags and placed them next to her on the metal grate.

Everyone left the lab and entered either the waiting room or the control room. Pearl could see her family and friends in the observation window above her. They were all smiling as the hum of the machine started up.

Kyle's voice came through the speakers. "See you on the other side, Pearl. Good luck."

The platform began to ascend into the glass dome. It reached its destination and locked into place.

Connor walked over to the circuit dials. He switched the machine over to its dual setting: time travel and teleportation. This would send Pearl not only to the date and time they wanted, but the city as well.

Connor spun each dial until it read: April 10, 1912; 10:00 AM; Southampton, England.

The machine quieted down as it prepared to fire up. The hum began to grow as Pearl caught Sam's gaze. He raised a hand and held it there. Pearl returned the gesture as they smiled at each other. Sam opened his mouth and mouthed the words, *I love you.*

Pearl was caught off-guard, but somehow was not surprised by his sudden declaration of feelings.

I love you, Pearl responded as Connor turned the machine on.

The hum began again and increased in pitch as the dischargers began to glow. Electricity shot out of the dischargers and into the conducting wires, shooting into the pool of water.

Pearl's friends had described the sensation of the transcribing process to her before, but she could never have imagined what it really felt like. It did not hurt exactly; it was just a tingle. It was as if every cell in her body was vibrating against each other. At this point, Pearl knew the electrical currents were traveling through her body, scattering cells and molecules.

Pearl felt a small sense of panic run through her, but reined it in. The electricity would not harm her; the process had been engineered to jolt the agent into the space-time continuum, but not to denature any enzymes or other cells. The water under the metal grate began to swirl faster and faster until it started to swirl into the air, creating a cocoon around Pearl.

The water was used for its ability to disperse electricity. With the electrical currents connecting to every fiber of Pearl's being, the electricity would not only de-atomize the hydrogen and oxygen, but it would de-atomize her own cells as well.

The cocoon enveloped Pearl, shielding her from the outside world. Miniature electrical impulses jumped between the water droplets like lightning bolts in a rainstorm.

Pearl gazed through the curtain of water, watching the lab shimmer in front of her. The artificial lights of the lab grew steadily until they changed into sunlight, shining down from a blue sky. The lab tables disappeared, replaced by people in dresses and suits. The walls crumbled around her to reveal an expanse of dock and sky. Pearl looked up at the observation area to watch as it transformed into a ship that loomed larger than life in front of her. As the scene appeared in front of her, the world went white.

One final surge of electricity broke down her physiology and scattered her cells into the currents. The electricity was drawn into the copper, gold and stainless steel conductors and pulled down into the water tank. The copper and gold were used as conductors, and the stainless steel was used to disperse the currents.

The tank shone with electricity as a beam of light was directed into the diamond. The diamond shone like a prism before shooting back up into the pool of water. Water shot towards the ceiling, releasing the organic molecules into the atmosphere. As the light faded and the water fell back to the pool, the date on the timeline under the tank started to glow. The machine shut down as the date went back to normal:

April 10, 1912

6

Ship of Dreams

Pearl landed with a thud behind some crates. She took a second to right herself and stood up. She could hear a crowd in the dock, cheering. A tremendous horn blew from the cruise liner that awaited its passengers. She pulled the video camera out and started recording herself.

"Okay," she said. "I've just arrived in the dock at Southampton...April 10, 1912. And I'm about to get my first look at the *Titanic.*"

Pearl placed the glasses on her face so it could see what she saw. She made sure she had the tickets, her luggage, and most importantly, her pendant before she cautiously made her way around the crates. The sight that met her eyes was astounding. Hundreds upon hundreds of people gathered in the dock, either boarding or watching the R.M.S. *Titanic*.

The ship itself was majestic. Pearl could practically hear the escalating music from the movie in her mind. It was bigger than she could have ever imagined. The movie did not do it justice. Sure, it was grand on the movie, but that was just a two-dimensional figure. It's so different when you actually see it in person. It was right here and larger than life. The sheer splendor of it all tugged a couple of heartstrings inside Pearl. Her face split into a wide grin as she thought about what awaited her inside.

The black, white and red paint of the iron hull shone new and brilliant in the sun. The yellow letters written on the bow spoke of grandeur and majesty. No rust had tarnished the keel; no corrosion, no barnacles—only the pristine splendor of a new master of the sea. Its white railings remained undamaged—no paint peeling, no dents. The portholes sparkled like diamonds as the sun reflected its brilliance in the glass. The funnels stood erect on the Boat Deck—four tan and black skyscrapers that billowed steam from their mouths.

At the stern, a red, two-pointed flag with a white star emblazoned on it fluttered in the breeze. The small, white lifeboats sat silently along the edges of the Boat Deck, standing guard over their mighty captain as she waited for her passengers. The bow pointed toward open water, as though the ship itself was eager to begin her journey into the open ocean. Seagulls bustled about in front of the ship, basking in the morning air.

The infamous scene was, in itself, so surreal that it would take nothing short of a blow to the head to forget that moment. Every picture she had ever seen of the *Titanic* made the ship look old and faded. Seeing the ship now in real life, she practically roared of color and novelty. Pearl wanted to gaze in wonder at the beautiful sight in front of her, but knew that the *Titanic* would not wait for her.

Pearl looked at the old watch the agency had given her. It was ten o'clock, and the *Titanic* left at noon; she had two hours to get onboard.

Pearl's first stop was the health inspection. Since the agency needed a full report, they had to ensure that Pearl would not be put onto a lifeboat because she was a first-class woman. She was perfectly capable of getting off of the lifeboat, but what kind of sane person would jump back onto a sinking ship? So, the agency had given her a third-class ticket so she would stay on. Also, the first-class passengers were very high profile. A third-class passenger could go unnoticed.

They had an agreement, however. If she was in danger of hypothermia, she would use the pendant right then. She had been urged to stay as long as she could, but if it became life-threatening, she had no choice.

Pearl finally found the health inspection queue and got into line. About fifteen minutes later, she looked at the cars approaching the dock. Passengers were arriving from all over England, smiles on their eager faces. The papers and media had exalted the liner, even making the claim that God Himself could not sink her.

Maybe not, but the iceberg will, Pearl thought, snickering inwardly at the irony of it all.

She immediately reprimanded herself for joking about it. People had lost their lives, loved ones and possessions because of this tragedy. It was definitely not a laughing matter at all.

"Miss," came a voice in front of her.

Pearl turned to see the health inspector waiting for her.

"Sorry," she said.

Pearl stepped forward and let her hair down so they could comb through it for lice. The inspection took about ten minutes. When they were done checking for lice, they checked her teeth, her ears, her nails, her clothes and her eyes to make sure she had no diseases. Pearl picked up her luggage and headed for the baggage check. The line took about another fifteen minutes to get through.

Pearl headed to the loading dock and got her ticket out. She climbed onto the gangway to the third-class entryway on E Deck at the stern and followed the man in front of her.

A ticket checker stood just inside the door. As Pearl made her way towards him, his face brightened. Obviously, he was getting bored with his job. After all, he had been here for more than two hours.

Pearl stopped in front of the man, holding her ticket in her hand.

You can still turn back, a voice in the back of Pearl's head told her. *You don't have to go through this.*

I have to, Pearl thought back.

At least warn Lachlan and Constance. You could save their lives.

But then I might not exist.

Who cares? You could save them any pain. You could prolong their lives...give Sean the life he never had.

But I must not interfere.

"Miss?" asked the ticket checker.

Pearl slowly handed over her ticket as the words of Hockley from the trailer of *Titanic* rang in her ears:

"I pulled every string I could to book us on the grandest ship in history, and you act as if you're going to your execution."

The ticket checker looked over her ticket and handed it back.

One foot at a time, Pearl entered the doomed ship. Even though the disaster was still five days away, she could feel the *Titanic*'s fate bearing down on her. She tried to tell herself that it was not real, but at the same time, the gnawing sense pervaded her that it was all happening here and now.

Pearl looked at her ticket for her room number and began searching for it. She noticed it was on G Deck, so she walked down the corridor and turned right into a short corridor. She passed through an open gate and headed for the staircase on her right. Pearl carefully made her way down the staircase two decks, arriving on G Deck. At the bottom of the staircase, she turned right, heading down a small hallway. Pearl looked at the numbers on the doors, heading right down a narrow corridor all the way to the end.

Pearl's room was a two-berth third-class room right up against the keel below the waterline. There was no one else in her room, and she knew no one would be joining her. The agency wanted as little interference as possible with the passengers, so they found her an empty room.

Pearl entered, setting her things in the room. She took a moment once her hands were empty and looked around the room.

It was a simple room with only the necessities: one small bed in the corner with a small closet in the other corner and a small wash basin along one wall. Pearl stared at the sheets on the bed, noticing how new and pristine they looked.

Everything on this ship was brand new and never been used. She and the others would be the first to use everything…the first and only.

She got her journal out and began writing about her journey so far. She relaxed for a while before she decided to head to the deck for cast-off.

~~

Thomas Andrews, the architect for the Harland & Wolff shipyard, walked onto the bridge, watching Captain Edward John Smith assemble his crew for the launch of the maiden voyage. Captain Smith noticed Andrews by the entryway and nodded at him. Andrews returned the nod with a smile and spotted Joseph Bruce Ismay, the chairman of the White Star Line, walking onto the bridge through the opposite entryway.

"Thomas," greeted Ismay as he approached him, shaking his hand.

"Mr. Ismay," replied Andrews in a gentle Irish accent. "Wondurful day fur a voyage, yes?"

"Absolutely," said Ismay, glancing at the bow through the forward windows. "We have wonderful weather, plenty of sunshine, favorable wind, calm waters…God is surely smiling on us."

"Surely," said Andrews, smiling at that sentiment.

"E.J.!" called Ismay gently.

Captain Smith turned and approached Ismay.

"I trust everything is going swimmingly?" Ismay inquired.

Captain Smith smiled. "It couldn't be going better. Everything is right on schedule."

"No concerns?" Andrews asked Smith seriously.

Captain Smith shook his head briefly. "None. It is all going better than anticipated. We couldn't have asked for anything better."

"Excellent," commended Ismay. "Excellent. How long until we're underway?"

Smith pulled out his pocket watch, looking at the time. "Launch is at twelve o'clock. We have approximately thirty minutes until then. Shouldn't be long now."

"Good, good," said Ismay, exiting the bridge with Andrews.

~~

Pearl began heading down the narrow corridor the way she came, turning left towards the staircase that brought her down. Reaching E Deck, Pearl turned right and headed aft down a corridor and through a gate, reaching the third-class main staircase. She headed up to C Deck, heading through a door in front of her.

Pearl walked through the door and emerged in the aft well deck. She headed for the staircase on her right and walked up to the stern deck, also known as the fantail. She rushed over to the port railing, gazing down at the people in the dock. They were waving and blowing kisses to their friends and family onboard.

Pearl looked around at the passengers on the deck with her. Everyone was leaning over the railings and waving goodbye, positively thrilled to be headed to America.

Pearl spotted several third-class passengers on the dock. They rushed by next to the ship, waving their tickets. A couple of firemen and stokers soon joined them. They had the misfortune of arriving late for the voyage, unknowingly giving themselves the fortune of missing the disaster.

Among these lucky few was Thomas Hart. He had been mugged at a bar after a drinking binge, and his discharge book—which was a crewman's identification in these days—was stolen by an unknown man, who boarded the *Titanic* as a fireman in Hart's stead. Ashamed about the ordeal, Hart did not mention it to anyone and left town for a while. Three weeks after the sinking of the *Titanic*, Hart would return home to his family—who had been notified of his death—with a smile on his face, causing his mother to pass out and nearly suffer a heart attack.

Pearl turned her camera on and filmed the crowd down below.

Since the technology in 1912 was too simple for a camera that Pearl needed, the company designed it to be disguised as a pair of spectacles. The spectacles were a simple design for the decade of 1910. It was designed to withstand a lot of pressure and force for the sinking, yet it had to be something a woman in 1912 could wear with anything. Pearl could wear them on her face to film whatever she was seeing, or remove them in order to film herself. She had to be sure that no one was around when she talked to the camera, though.

Right now, the glasses sat on the bridge of her nose. She turned the camera onto the passengers on the ship. Seamen began untying the ship from the dock, and Pearl started filming them.

As they drew the giant ropes onto the deck, an old couple found their way to the railing beside Pearl. She turned to look at them as they waved to people down below and hugged each other, smiling. Pearl's eyes welled up with tears as the couple embraced each other.

These people, especially the third-class passengers, were so happy and thrilled to be on the grandest ship afloat. They had probably saved up for months, maybe even years, to have enough money for a Trans-Atlantic voyage. Now, they had the apparent luck to be booked on the *Titanic*, traveling in the lap of luxury, even in steerage. The third-class passengers had boarded the ship, looking forward to a new life in a new country. However, for many, their new lives would be tragically cut short before they could arrive in their new home.

A loud whistle blew, startling Pearl a little. Apparently, the whistle told everyone for miles that the *Titanic* was setting out on her maiden voyage. The ship was allowed to drift away from the dock as the tugboats pulled out in front. Pearl had her camera pointed towards the front of the ship to film *Titanic*'s departure.

There was a slight rumble beneath Pearl's feet. She rushed over to the stern railing and pointed her glasses at the water. It was still and calm, but the water started churning as the propellers began to spin. Pretty soon, a tremendous wake had generated.

Pearl glanced over at the dock and saw it slowly go by. The second that the stern was clear of the dock, Pearl let out a deep breath.

"Well..." Pearl muttered to herself as a tear formed in her eye. "We're officially at sea."

A male steerage passenger noticed her and turned to her with a beaming face.

"Don't worry," he told her in a deep British accent. "We'll see these shores again someday."

Pearl looked at him sadly.

That's what Sam said, she thought.

She smiled feebly at the young lad. "Yeah...we will..."

The man turned back to the beautiful view sailing past them.

Pearl turned and looked at all the passengers with her. On her own deck, men laughed with each other about being on such a great ship. Women talked quietly with each other. Children ran around playing games and interacting with their parents.

Pearl gazed further up into the upper decks and watched the first and second-class passengers. Most were still at the railings, looking down at the water below. Some were talking animatedly among themselves. The men all wore their Sunday best: fine suits with bowler hats and walking canes.

The women's dresses were colorful, shiny and richly decorated. There were blues, reds, greens, yellows, purples, blacks, pinks and even a strange orange dress. The colors were all pastels and light colors; the women saved the really glamorous dresses for dinner parties. All the ladies wore hats that matched their dresses accompanied with matching gloves. Most were escorted by a man except for a rare few that were alone.

Children did not race around on these decks. Instead, they played with sophisticated toys or just stood around with their parents and looked rich.

As *Titanic* approached another dock, Pearl rushed back to the port side. She could see the *New York* and the *Oceanic* moored to a nearby dock. As the *Titanic* drew near, Pearl's breath caught in her chest. The ship drew abreast the other two, and Pearl looked over the railing at the water below.

Waves spread like ripples away from the iron belly of the leviathan and spread towards the *New York*. The ship began to bounce in the wake of the *Titanic*. The *Oceanic* that the *New York* was moored to followed suit. They rocked inversely; as the *New York* went up, the *Oceanic* went down.

Finally, the six mooring lines could not take the strain and snapped at the stern of the *New York*.

BANG!

The sound was like the sharp report of a pistol, causing several people to cry out in alarm.

The ship began to drift towards the *Titanic*'s stern, drawn in by the suction. Several passengers around Pearl gasped or shouted in alarm. She looked down at the tugboat *Vulcan* as it raced towards the *New York* to intercept her.

The *New York* continued to drift straight for them as the *Titanic* shut her engines down. The *Vulcan* positioned itself between the *New York* and the *Titanic* and swung a line over the stern. The first line missed, so the sailors threw a second line over, which caught on the stern of the smaller vessel. The two ships were now a mere four feet away from colliding. The little tugboat then began to steam away from the *Titanic*, pulling the *New York* slowly along with it.

By now, the *Titanic* had started to steam full astern to avoid a collision. There was a relative sigh of relief onboard as a major disaster was avoided.

It would've been better if it was hit here than out on the ocean, Pearl thought. *All those people could have been saved.*

"This is a good omen!" a female passenger cried out. "It means it is the worst trouble we will encounter on the voyage!"

Several people nodded their agreement, but Pearl was not fooled.

No, she thought. *It's a sign of things to come...things much worse.*

7

First-Class Wonders

Once the disaster had been averted, the *Titanic* was cleared for a second departure. An hour later, the ship began moving once more on her twenty-four mile journey across the English Channel. The passengers had long since gone to their rooms below decks. Pearl followed suit and arrived at her private room in less than ten minutes. Pearl had turned off her camera, stowing the glasses in their case. She walked over to the iron wall of her room.

Her room was set up right next to the hull, and Pearl knew that her room was also below the waterline. She walked over to the hull and placed a hand on the wall. The metal hummed slightly under her hand, and she thought of the water just outside the riveted iron plates, pressing against the hull to gain entry into the forbidden space inside.

Pearl took a moment to bond with the past.

The history and legend right in front of me, Pearl thought, running a hand down the iron wall. *And it's right here...in real life.*

Pearl walked over to her bed and plopped down on it. From under her clothes, she pulled the heart locket out and unclasped it. She held it in her hand and smiled. She opened the locket and found a picture in it.

It was a picture of Pearl and Sam the day they had gone to the fair. They had climbed into one of the photo booths together. The picture in the locket was the picture they had placed their heads together, cheek to cheek, folded in each other's arms. Both of them were looking up at Pearl out of the photo and were smiling. Pearl laughed as she put the locket back around her neck.

She sat up and looked at her watch: 2:00 p.m. Pearl opened one of her bags and sifted carefully through the first-class dresses until she found one she liked: an emerald-green satin dress with black lace on the top portion. She pulled the whole thing on with some difficulty and put her hair up. She got out some make-up and applied it. She stared at her reflection until she was satisfied.

As Pearl pulled a cloak out of her bag, she also retrieved her camera. She placed it on the top of her dress at her chest, one of the earpieces tucked between the satin and her skin, and wrapped the cloak around her, making sure to cover up all of her dress. She opened her door and entered the hallway.

There were a few people milling about, but most were still up top on the decks, enjoying the last of the sunlight. It was three o'clock now, and the sun would be setting in a few hours.

Pearl walked up the main staircase towards the upper decks. She emerged out of a door, and sunlight hit her face. She was in the aft well deck facing the bow of the ship. She looked up towards the Boat Deck and saw some officers walking the decks. As they would pass each other, they would nod their heads slightly.

Pearl walked to the port railing and looked out at the land at the bow and the stern: England behind them, France in front of them. The shores were quite a bit away; they were only about halfway across the channel. According to the history books, the *Titanic* would dock a few miles from shore at Cherbourg at 6:30 p.m. They still had three and a half hours.

Pearl walked over to the starboard railing and gazed at the horizon. She could see England on the right and France on the left. Beyond the shores, Pearl could see open sea. The words of Rose echoed in her ears:

"By the next afternoon, we were sailing from the coast of Ireland with nothing out ahead of us but ocean."

Pearl breathed in the sweet sea air and smiled. She walked over to the staircase that lead to B Deck and took her cloak off, stowing it in a secure place behind the stairs.

Pearl came to the foot of the stairs and walked past the staircase, heading into a doorway that would lead forward toward the bow. She walked past the second-class library and into the first-class starboard corridor. Walking the length of it, she headed towards the forward grand staircase.

An old couple passed by her, and Pearl recognized them: Isidor and Ida Straus. Pearl watched as they walked down the starboard C Deck corridor.

As Pearl passed by passengers, she could not help wondering: who would live and who would die? Was this man to be a lucky survivor? Had this little boy's time come? Would this woman be mourning the death of her husband in five days' time?

Pearl was so caught up in watching the passengers that she almost passed the forward grand staircase. She shook her head in amazement that she could have missed such a spectacular sight. She began ascending the stairs and approached the A Deck landing. She came around, stealing herself for her first look at the famous grand staircase. She rounded the corner and paused.

The sight was to die for.

The steps were made of marbled linoleum on the tops, wood on the vertical sides, with gold plating on the edges. Linoleum was a new invention at this time, and it was chosen because it was cheaper. The gold plating on the edges of the stairs was placed there to keep the linoleum from curling.

The oak paneling was intricately carved; a flourish of beautiful craftsmanship. The carvings seemed to make the wood pop out and come alive. The oak banisters were wide and finely polished, supported by wrought-iron balustrades inlaid with twenty-four karat carved gold.

A carved wooden image displayed "Honor and Glory Crowning Time" at the small landing halfway up the stairs. Between the two wooden figures, a clock read 3:30.

Pearl walked to the foot of the staircase and stared up into the glass dome. Light poured through it, illuminating the room and the elegant crystal chandelier at the very center of the dome. Black metal designs held the glass dome in place. White oak lined the bottom of the glass dome, popping out from the brown oak directly underneath it.

Pearl realized that her camera was not on, and she fumbled to put the glasses on and push the power switch. It started recording as Pearl walked up to the Boat Deck. She walked around the railing until she was opposite the Honor and Glory clock.

As Pearl marveled at the beauty, phrases from the movie thrust themselves into her mind:

*"From this moment, no matter what we do...*Titanic *will founder."*

"But this ship can't sink!"

"She's made of iron, sir. I assure you, she can...and she will. It is a mathematical certainty."

"The ship will sink...In an hour or so...all this will be at the bottom of the Atlantic."

"Half the people on this ship are going to die."[3]

Pearl turned off her camera and made her way back down the stairs towards the A Deck. She walked out to the promenade and headed aft. Resolving to spend some time in the Palm Court Café, she walked until she came to the sliding glass doors. Stewards opened the doors and greeted her as she walked inside.

Pearl found a small table in the corner that was empty and walked over to it. She sat down, and, within a couple minutes, a steward came

---

[3] From James Cameron's *"Titanic."*

over. He wore the standard steward uniform: black pants and shoes with a white, long-sleeved, gold-buttoned tunic.

"Care for anything, miss?" he asked.

"I'll have a cup of tea," Pearl told him with the air of a high society member.

The steward nodded and left.

Pearl looked around at the people around her. She recognized a few passengers, but most were random faces. Most were deep in conversation, enjoying their afternoon tea.

"Here is your tea, miss," the waiter said as he placed the china cup in front of her.

"Thank you," Pearl told him as she took the teaspoon and stirred it.

"Traveling by yourself?" asked a small feminine voice.

Pearl glanced up to look at the woman at the table across from her. The woman wore a pink pastel floral dress and pearl earrings. She had turned around and was facing Pearl. Pearl stared as she recognized the woman.

"Yes," Pearl answered, trying to get a grip on her stunned expression.

"So am I," the woman answered. She stood up and walked over to Pearl's table. "Cecily Miles."

Pearl smiled, gesturing to the empty chair adjacent to her own. "Pearl Liberti."

Cecily sat down next to Pearl and smiled. She looked at the locket around Pearl's neck.

"That is lovely," she said. "Who gave it to you?"

"My husband," Pearl told her. "He said it was to remember him by while I was away from him."

"What is his name?" Cecily asked.

Pearl responded with the first name that came into her head, the name of the man she had come to hope would be her husband some day.

"Samuel."

"Samuel…" Cecily mused. "That is a strong name. What does he do for a living?"

"He's the owner of a small company for historical records…What about you? Do you have anyone special?"

Cecily shook her head ever so slightly. "That is why I am going to America. Maybe then I can find myself a husband."

"Well, in that case, I wish you luck."

Pearl took a sip of tea and smiled at Cecily.

~~

Captain Edward John Smith walked up to the railing that overlooked the bow of the *Titanic*. In a day's time, they would be heading out to sea. Smith felt honored to captain such a majestic ship before retiring.

In the distance, France awaited them as they steamed along at a steady speed.

Second Officer Charles Lightoller approached Smith with his pocket watch out and open.

"Four o'clock, sir," Lightoller reported. "We are to dock at Cherbourg in approximately two and one half hours."

"An hour late..." Smith muttered to himself. He paused for a second. "Very good, Mr. Lightoller."

"Sir," Lightoller responded and headed for the bridge.

Smith stood at the railing for a while, staring at the shoreline ahead. He thought about what had happened in Southampton because of the *Titanic*'s wake.

"Doomed before we even start," Smith muttered to himself.

No matter how many times he tried to convince himself, he could not get rid of that nagging feeling of foreboding. Smith resolved at that moment that he would do all in his power to reach New York in safety.

8

Dinner in Style

Pearl grabbed the cloak she had stowed under the stairwell and wrapped it around her. After she talked with Cecily, she had enjoyed the warm sea air until 5:00 p.m. Now, she was headed to her room to change for dinner.

She opened the door to her room and placed the cloak on the bed. She picked out a black satin-and-lace dress that had a black headpiece. By the time she had finally gotten into her dress, it was six o'clock.

"No wonder all the women had maids," Pearl huffed as she finally managed to pin the last of her hair into place.

Pearl transferred the pendant from her green dress to the inside pocket in the black dress. She placed the glasses on her face and the locket around her neck. She grabbed her cloak and draped it over her head, taking care to cover up the fancy beads and black silk.

As Pearl checked herself in the mirror, she thought about Sam.

"Wish you were here, Sam," Pearl whispered. "It would've been great."

She opened the door and strolled into the corridor. She encountered very few people on the way to the well deck, as everyone was on their way to dinner right now.

At 6:30, the passengers boarding at Cherbourg would join them in their voyage. Pearl knew that the passengers would board and the *Titanic* would then turn to the west and head for Queenstown, Ireland.

As Pearl opened the door to the well deck and stepped into the evening air, the lights of the ship shone beautifully in the dusk. Pearl stowed her cloak under the staircase once again and made her way towards the grand staircase.

Pearl had no trouble remembering the way; the decks and passageways were becoming second nature. Pretty soon, she would be able to walk the ship blindfolded. Of course, knowing the ship like the back of her hand also came with its disadvantages. It would just make it that much harder to say goodbye. Pearl knew that, before long, *Titanic* would become like an old companion, and it would grow harder to remain neutral.

Pearl faintly heard three blows of the ship's whistle from above, signaling the liner's departure from Cherbourg. It meant that all the Cherbourg passengers were now onboard, and the ship was ready for castoff.

Pearl reached the grand staircase and looked into the well in front of her. The scene never failed to amaze her; this was beginning to become her favorite place on the ship.

Pearl walked down to the D Deck landing, accompanied by other well-dressed passengers. As Pearl watched the people around her, someone touched her gently on her shoulder. Pearl turned and smiled, surprised to see Cecily Miles in front of her.

"Hello again," Cecily said. She turned to her three female companions. "Girls, I'd like you to meet Pearl Liberti."

"Hello," Pearl smiled at them.

The three other women were dressed to impress. One woman with blonde hair wore a royal blue dress that covered her shoulders and rippled out from her body. She had ivory skin with eyes that were a brilliant blue. She looked to be around twenty years old.

The next woman had brown hair and looked very delicate. She wore a pink gown that was covered in a white lace covering. She also had ivory skin, but her eyes were green.

The third woman also had blonde hair, but her skin was a pale tan, and her eyes were brown. She wore a scarlet gown whose black covering trailed a couple of inches behind her.

Cecily herself had her black hair up under a white feather that stuck out of the back. Her dress was a brilliant white that ran down to her feet.

"Pearl," Cecily went on as she gestured towards the brunette, "this is Helen Candee. She is a well-known author." She gestured to the blonde with ivory skin and blue eyes. "This is Malvina Cornell. Her husband founded Cornell University. And this is Edith Rosenbaum. She is a fashion correspondent."

The tan blonde nodded curtly at Pearl.

Cecily spotted someone behind Pearl. "Ah! Pearl, there is someone you absolutely have to meet."

She headed off through the crowd with Pearl resolutely following her.

As Cecily drew nearer to the newcomer, Pearl caught sight of a man that she recognized. He escorted a woman that looked about five months pregnant. Pearl watched as John Jacob Astor and his wife Madeleine interacted with the other first-class guests.

"Hello, my dear," Cecily was saying to her friend. "You look splendid tonight. I have someone to introduce to you. Pearl, this is Mr. J. Bruce Ismay."

Pearl turned to face the prosperous chairman of the White Star Line, brandishing a smile as she did so.

Joseph Bruce Ismay was a statuesque middle-aged man who stood tall, radiating confidence and competence. He exuded excellence and seemed to know it. Pearl would guess that Ismay's self-perception consisted of a prima donna worldview.

"Hello, Miss..." began Ismay, indicating that Cecily had not introduced Pearl by her last name.

"Liberti," said Pearl, holding her hand daintily forward.

"Pleasure to meet you, miss," Ismay greeted as he grasped her hand, bending his spine forward to kiss her hand.

"The pleasure is all mine," Pearl said as Ismay gently released her hand. "I understand that you are the owner of the White Star Line."

"Chairman, actually," Ismay corrected. "J.P. Morgan and I own the company together, but I wouldn't put the sole possession on my shoulders."

"But it was still your idea to build and market these wonderful Olympic-class ships," Pearl went on, playing on his ego.

Ismay smiled cordially. "Why, yes, it was. In fact, *Titanic* is the largest, most luxurious man-made object on the seas."

Pearl took an admiring look at their impressive surroundings. "I believe it. She truly is remarkable; the finest in all of history."

"Why, thank you," said Ismay. He looked over at a group of passengers about fifteen feet from them. "If you would excuse me."

"Of course," said Pearl, letting Ismay return to his party-going and hand-wringing. Pearl looked up at Cecily, who was waiting for her to finish her conversation with the chairman. "You know everyone, don't you?"

"Oh, that was nothing," said Cecily. "I have someone else to introduce to you." She turned to the woman behind her. "Pearl, this is Margaret Brown."

Pearl froze as she heard the name. She slowly looked up at the woman behind Cecily and came face-to-face with the gold mining heiress known today as Molly Brown. She wore a black dress sequined with black beads and black lace. Her hair had been done up in an elegant bun. Margaret smiled at Pearl as she took her in.

"Hello, honey," Margaret said as she extended her hand.

"Pearl Liberti," Pearl told her. "It's a pleasure to meet you, Mrs. Brown."

"Oh, please," smiled Margaret. "Call me Margaret."

Pearl smiled. "Margaret. What brings you to the *Titanic*?"

"I am returning to my home in America after a holiday in Egypt," Margaret replied. "I was eager to make the same trip with the Astors. Isn't Madeleine just a doll?"

Pearl laughed politely. "Oh, yes, she is."

Margaret looked over Pearl's shoulder, spotting someone. "Hey, Astor!" She looked back at Pearl. "Speaking of the Astors, I've just spotted John. I'll see you later, dearie."

"I'll see you," said Pearl, letting Margaret run off to converse with John Jacob Astor.

Cecily smiled at Pearl. "You seem to get along with everyone you meet."

"It's a gift," said Pearl, watching as Cecily's earlier three female friends returned to their side. "If you ladies will excuse me."

"Have a wonderful evening, Pearl," said Cecily.

"And to you as well," Pearl concluded.

Cecily turned to her friends as Pearl turned away from them.

Pearl left Cecily and approached the doors to search the crowd. Her eyes fell on a figure near a table in the center of the dining saloon. The man was dressed in a suit and overcoat, his face kind and young.

Pearl approached the table, leaning towards the man. "Mr. Andrews?"

Thomas Andrews, *Titanic*'s designer and architect, turned and smiled at Pearl, speaking in a gentle Irish accent. "Yes, madam?"

"I thought that was you," Pearl told him with a smile, holding her hand out delicately. "I am Pearl Liberti."

"Pleasure t' meet you, Miss Liberti," Andrews told her, taking her hand and placing a kiss on her fingers as he bowed slightly. "How may I help you?"

"I am employed with the *Daily Herald*," Pearl explained. "It's our first issue.[4] My article will be written on the structure of this wonderful ship. I was wondering if you would be able to give me a tour of the ship."

"Ah, a tour," mused Andrews, a smile playing onto his face. "What would you like t' see?"

"Would it be possible to see the bridge, forecastle, Marconi Room and engine room?"

Andrews seemed to mull it over. "Yes...yes, I think that would be doable. I can give you a tour on Monday afternoon before dinner. How does that sound?"

No, Pearl thought. *Monday afternoon does not sound good at all. It's kind of hard to tour a sunken ship.*

Pearl thought for a moment, wondering how to persuade him otherwise.

"Actually, I was hoping to take a tour on Sunday so I am able to write my article while I am on the ship," Pearl told him. "I would like to get the article to the paper as soon as I can."

"Hm," Andrews deliberated, his brow furrowing. "I am available immediately after Sunday morning mass. Will that work for you?"

"Yes, thank you," Pearl replied gratefully. "I appreciate it."

She began to walk away.

---

4 The *Daily Herald*'s first issue was published April 15, 1912, featuring the sinking of the *Titanic*.

"Miss?" Andrews called.

Pearl turned and smiled at the naval architect. "Yes?"

"Would you care t' join us?" Andrews asked. "Unless you have your own party t' tend t'."

"Why, thank you," said Pearl. "I would love to join you."

Pearl followed Andrews to one of the larger tables in the center of the dining room. People had already assembled themselves around it, awaiting the start of dinner. There were twelve seats to this table, and a passenger occupied every seat.

Pearl would be joining Thomas Andrews, Joseph Bruce Ismay, Charles Melville Hays and his wife Clara, Major Archibald Gracie, Cosmo Duff Gordon and his wife Lucile, the Countess of Rothes, and Doctor Washington Dodge with his wife Ruth and four-year-old son Washington, Jr.

"Everyone, I would like you t' meet Pearl Liberti," Andrews introduced her to the group. "She is a reporter for the *Daily Herald*."

Everyone made their own greetings heard, and Pearl and Andrews settled down at the table with them to begin dinner.

9

Sunrises and Maiden Voyages

Pearl walked into the enclosure that housed the grand staircase. She was on the Boat Deck level, dressed in a beautiful white dress. It was a light silk, and it was ornately decorated with diamonds. She wore a white feather in her hair and lace gloves.

She walked over to the staircase leading to the clock landing and looked across the way to see a man in a brilliant tuxedo looking at her.

"Sam..." Pearl whispered.

Sam smiled as he began descending the stairs. Pearl did the same, and they met in the middle. Sam held his hand out, and Pearl placed hers in it. He lowered his face and kissed her hand. He let her hand go and held his bent elbow out.

Pearl gently placed her hand in the crook of his elbow, and together, they descended the stairs to A Deck. Level after level, they went down arm-in-arm. *As they passed the candelabra at the D Deck landing, the passengers around them slowly faded away. The tables and chairs disappeared, and the tableware went with them.*

Sam let go of Pearl's arm and bowed, offering his hand. Pearl took it as she curtsied. They took hold of each other's hands, and Pearl placed her other one on his shoulder. As music began to swell, Sam wrapped his arm around the small of Pearl's back.

They began to dance slowly as a waltz struck up from an invisible band. For a while, they waltzed until the music suddenly changed, becoming a festive jig.

Pearl smiled as she kicked off her shoes. Sam grabbed her by the hands, and they started dancing to the fast-paced Irish music. They were dancing all over the floor, having a fun time. Pearl wrapped her arms around Sam's neck, laughing as he embraced her and spun her around.

Something started beeping; it was shrill and rapid, and it came from all around them. Sam set Pearl down, and she looked up at him with confusion on her face.

The room around them began to change once again, this time for the worse. The walls began to decay and crumble, the floor became buried in silt and sand, the staircase behind them disintegrated and disappeared altogether, and the lights dimmed until the room was bathed in a faint, eerie blue glow.

Pearl looked in confusion at the shipwreck around them, wondering what was happening. She looked back up at Sam, searching for answers.

Sam leaned down and brushed his lips against her cheek. He brought his head back and looked down at her as the beeping grew louder.

Pearl opened her eyes as the beeping grew louder. Flinging her hand over, she grasped the digital watch hooked to the bedrail. She turned the alarm off and looked at the time: 6:00 a.m. *Titanic*'s first sunrise was in forty-five minutes.

Pearl climbed out of bed and approached the sink in the room. She stripped and bathed herself by the sink, since third-class rooms did not come with bathtubs. Deciding to save washing her hair for later, she proceeded to dress herself in a third-class dress: brown cotton with a simple plaid shawl. She also grabbed her cloak to keep herself warm in the cold morning breeze. She put her glasses on, hid the locket under her top, and opened the door to her cabin.

Almost nobody was awake at this hour, so Pearl encountered only the occasional crew member as she headed down the corridor and climbed the stairs.

As she headed out the door and into the aft well deck, she spared a glimpse at the lightening sky. Portside, the sky still held the lingering traces of night, with the moon still visible near the horizon. Pearl headed to the starboard railing, leaning against it. The sky lightened from a navy to a sea blue to a robin's egg blue the further east it went.

Pearl inhaled a great lungful of sea air, closing her eyes and taking in the moment. She knew that disaster lay only four days away, but she reveled in the peaceful moment.

The *Titanic* remained most known for its sinking, but this right here…this was what it was all about. The largest ship in the world, the most beautiful, the most grand, the most luxurious liner was embarking on its maiden voyage. The *Titanic* was not about loss and tragedy. It was about perfection, purity and innocence.

That was *Titanic*'s legacy.

Pearl looked up at the sky once again. A yellow glow sat on the horizon, welcoming the day. Pearl switched the glasses on and watched the day unfold itself. Fluffy, pink cumulus clouds scattered themselves across the morning sky. The sky had lightened almost entirely to a sky blue as the sun approached.

Light hit Pearl's face suddenly, and she narrowed her eyes. A blinding disk had risen above the horizon, half-buried in the sea. The amber light hit the clouds, turning them from pink to orange. Sunlight bounced off of the waves, creating a mirror of light that danced over the ship.

Pearl looked back towards port, watching as the moon slowly sank towards the horizon. Pearl faced the front of the ship, the sun on her right and the moon on her left. For this one brief moment, it felt as though the whole universe was connected as the sun and moon competed for dominance in the spring sky. The sun won out and rose steadily into the sky, shining through the clouds ahead of them and illuminating small pockets of ocean in the distance. It appeared to be a giant spotlight, lighting their way.

Pearl turned and headed back down towards her room. It was 7:15, which meant that she had plenty of time to wash her hair in the sink and let it dry. Having a private room came with its advantages: she could use shampoo to wash her hair, since she was fairly certain real shampoo did not exist in 1912. Also, people at this time believed it

101

was not healthy to bathe every day, so they just gave themselves sponge baths. Pearl did not want to go a whole week without bathing.

While Pearl waited for her hair to dry, she wrote in her journal and went over the day's events. It looked like April 11 was a pretty hectic day, at least for the first half of it. Today was the day that they docked at Queenstown and then set sail for the Atlantic.

After reviewing her schedule and schematics, she put her hair up and changed into a first-class dress. In order to be on the B Deck promenade to watch the passengers board, she had to be a first-class woman.

Pearl wrapped her cloak around her dress and exited her room, heading up the staircase at the end of the corridor to E Deck. She walked down the corridor, through four open gates, and down a corridor commonly known as "Scotland Road." Halfway down the corridor, she came to a main staircase and headed down one deck, arriving at the third-class dining saloon.

It was 9:15, and breakfast was being served at that time. Pearl sat down and waited to be served.

~~

Forty-five minutes later, Pearl rose from her chair and approached the main third-class staircase, heading up to E Deck. She turned right down the "Scotland Road" and came upon a door to a smaller staircase halfway down the hall. She descended the staircase to F Deck and walked through an open gate on her left.

The constant stair-climbing was becoming irksome. However, the watertight bulkheads that ran up to E Deck necessitated the staircases. She simply could not move through the corridors on F Deck.

Walking down a narrow corridor, she approached the door to the Turkish Baths on her left. She opened the door and walked into the swimming pool area.

The swimming bath was open to first-class passengers only, and women were allowed swimming time from ten o'clock until one o'clock.

Pearl walked into one of the changing cubicles and dressed herself in one of the blue one-piece suits that the passengers wore when in the swimming area. Pearl walked out of the stall and lowered herself into the pool via the small stairway leading down into it. She took her time to relax in the heated saltwater. It felt soothing to her already weary body.

Man, if this is what I feel like after only a day and a half, I hate to imagine what I'm going to feel like in four days.

Giving herself forty-five minutes to swim, she exited the pool and entered the changing cubicle where her dress awaited her. Changing back into the dress, she exited the Turkish Baths and headed for the small staircase, ascending to E Deck and walking around to the back of the staircase where the elevators were located.

The elevator steward smiled at her and opened the gate to one of the elevators that was on that deck at the time. "Good morning, miss. Destination?"

"A Deck, please," Pearl responded as she stepped into the lift.

The steward on E Deck closed the outside doors as the elevator steward closed the gate and joggled the switch to the "Up" position. The lift began rising, and in a few minutes, they had arrived on A Deck.

"Here you are, madam," said the steward as he opened the accordion gate.

"Thank you," said Pearl as the deck steward opened the outer doors.

Pearl exited the lift and walked around the staircase, heading for the door that led to the enclosed port promenade. Heading forward towards the bow, she came to a small staircase near the wall on the right. Descending to the forward starboard B Deck, she wrapped her cloak around her shoulders since the day was a bit chilly. She walked over to the forward railing, watching as Ireland drew closer. It was 11:00 a.m., and the *Titanic* anchored just off shore at 11:30.

Pearl stood at the railing, enjoying the morning sun as *Titanic* drew closer to the shore.

Two tenders, the *America* and the *Ireland*, waited in the harbor to moor next to the liner and unload the passengers and mail bags. Pearl knew that one tender would unload the mail bags and cargo in the aft well deck via the electric cranes located on B Deck, and the other tender would unload passengers into the forward well deck on the portside.

~~

By 11:45, the tenders had anchored themselves to the *Titanic*, and were beginning to unload passengers. A gangplank had been added, one end on the deck of the *America* and one end on the railing of the forward well deck. A small portable staircase had been placed in front of the gangplank to assist the passengers into the well deck.

Now, the passengers were making their way from the tender and onto the steamer. Pearl watched with bated breath for her great grandparents, unsure of where they would be in the line. It appeared that first-class passengers were being loaded first, so Pearl waited patiently for the second-class passengers to board after them. Finally, the third-class passengers were being escorted onto the ship.

One by one, the immigrants boarded, walking up the gangway and showing their tickets. After several dozen passengers, a young couple climbed onto the well deck, immediately drawing Pearl's attention. These were two people she recognized.

After hours of searching the company's archives, Pearl had finally found a photograph of a young couple whose names were unknown. Pearl spent a long while poring over that picture, finding familiar facial characteristics in the two strangers. It seemed there had been proof of the Dunleavy's existence this whole time; no one had ever thought to connect the legend to the photograph.

Looking at the couple in front of her now, Pearl had no doubt that these two were her great grandparents. Now that Pearl could see them in person, she noticed that she had inherited Constance's smile along with her vivid red hair. She looked down at the baby in Constance's arms, Sean Dunleavy—her grandfather.

Now that Pearl had caught a glimpse of her great grandparents, she turned and made her way towards the grand staircase. She headed down to D Deck to eat lunch, since it was now 12:45. She seated herself at one of the tables and proceeded to wait for a steward.

After the passengers from Queenstown boarded the ship, those who had traveled onboard to cross the English Channel would depart on the tenders. Among these lucky few to disembark in Queenstown would be Father Francis M. Browne.

Father Browne had taken the most famous photographs of the *Titanic* while he had been onboard. When he arrived in Queenstown, he took his camera ashore with him, unknowingly taking a piece of history to share with the world.

~~

At 1:15 p.m., Pearl left the first-class dining saloon and headed back up to A Deck by way of the grand staircase. She exited the enclosed area on the starboard side and walked down to the forward B Deck railing.

Pearl glanced at her watch. In ten minutes, the starboard anchor would be raised for the final time, and *Titanic* would make her way into the open ocean.

Pretty soon, the chain that was submerged halfway in the water began to move, heading back into the chain locker located on the forecastle deck. As soon as the anchor was sheathed in its home on the side of the hull, the engines started up, gently humming through the ship.

As the ship slowly made its turn towards port to head west for America, Pearl left the railing in front of her and walked aft, ascending and descending multiple staircases to arrive at the aft well deck. Wrapping her cloak tighter around herself, she climbed up to the fantail, approaching the stern railing among the many passengers bidding their home goodbye. She clasped onto the chilled metal in front of her, gazing into the distance.

As they pulled away from the Irish shore, the propellers produced a torrential wake that billowed out from under the stern like clouds blown about by the wind. Pearl stood at the railing of the stern, smiling as the thrum of the engines vibrated up to her through the metal skeleton of the *Titanic*.

The roar of the ocean below came to her on the air as it was churned by the thirty-eight ton propellers. The wind whistled as it breezed over the decks and through the masts and funnels. The American flag next to Pearl flapped lightly in the wind, adding a soft swooshing as the material brushed against itself.

Bagpipes began playing behind her, and she turned to see Eugene Daly sitting on a bench on the deck, playing "Erin's Lament" on the bagpipes. He was playing a lament as they left Ireland, knowing he would never see his homeland again. Many of those onboard would never see their homeland, or any land, again. In a way, Daly was playing a lament not only for the passengers, but for the *Titanic* on its first, and only, voyage.

The *Titanic*, after all, was only three years old. She had been "born" on March 31, 1909, when Harland & Wolff began construction on her keel. However, she had only been at sea for ten months, having been launched on May 31, 1911. Construction and outfitting had been finished March 31, 1912, three years to the date from when construction began. In reality, *Titanic* had only been in operation for eleven days, despite the fact that her keel was three years old. *Titanic* had still been so young when she met her end.

Pearl turned and headed towards the staircase as the mournful notes drifted over the brisk, sea air.

10

Full Speed Ahead

Edward John Smith walked out of the captain's quarters, adjusting his cap.

Quartermaster Robert Hitchens stood in the wheelhouse, steering them away from Ireland. There were only two other people on the bridge: a seaman and Fifth Officer Harold Lowe. The seaman was checking the compass in the binnacle and telling Lowe their heading. Lowe then wrote it into the logbook. Smith watched as they turned to look at him.

"Carry on, men," Smith commanded, watching as they returned to their work.

Captain Smith walked through the wheelhouse door and entered the bridge area. Sixth Officer James Moody nodded at him from his post. There were a few seamen doing their routine jobs, and as Smith glanced out onto the starboard bridge wing, he spotted First Officer William Murdoch standing at the railing.

Captain Smith walked out to join his first officer. He stepped onto the platform in front of the railing as Murdoch looked at him. He glanced out at the vast water before him; no land in sight with plenty of open ocean waiting for the great *Titanic* to enter its fathomless expanse of blue majesty for the first time.

"Time to see what she can do, Mr. Murdoch," Captain Smith stated as he looked at his first officer. "Full speed ahead."

"Yes, sir," said Murdoch as he turned and headed into the bridge. "All ahead full, Mr. Moody."

"Very good, sir," Moody replied as the telegraph could be heard spinning its message to the engine room.

~~

Chief Engineer Joseph Bell looked over at the telegraph, which had just rung to get his attention. The arrow on the readout was pointing to "Ahead: Full."

"All ahead full," he announced as he went to survey the engineers.

Another officer spun the telegram to "Ahead: Full." Doing this sent a message down to the boiler rooms.

Bell walked to his railing as the engines began to rotate faster.

~~

Chief Stoker Frederick Barrett glanced up at the green light that had started blinking. He turned to his team of stokers and trimmers.

"Alright, men!" Barrett ordered, shouting to be heard over the roar of the boilers. "We've got full ahead! Let's stoke 'em right up! Let's get moving now, lads!"

The stokers began shoveling more and more coal into the boiler dampers as the trimmers brought wheelbarrow after wheelbarrow to the twenty-nine boilers.

~~

Murdoch came back to the captain as he watched the forward pace of the ship.

"Twenty-one knots, sir," he informed Smith.

Captain Smith placed his hands on the railing as he smiled in pride at his majestic ship. She was performing as well as he had expected.

Since the beginning of the voyage, they had only had one problem, if you did not count the fire in coal bunker Number Six. The fire had started and was still burning as they made their way west. Captain Smith was not too worried about it, though; the fire was contained fairly well enough and would not spread. He had complete faith in his firemen and stokers. Someone would eventually put it out.

What occupied Smith's thoughts at the moment was the performance of the ship. The way the prow slid through the water, the wind silently whipping over the decks, the gentle hum of the engines below...it was as though the *Titanic* was trying not to disturb the peaceful nature of the deep.

As if to exemplify this melting of machine and nature, Smith gazed down at the bow to see several dolphins riding the ship's bow wave. They weaved their way in front of the *Titanic*, occasionally jumping out of the ocean in excitement.

Smith felt pride rise up inside of him: pride for the vessel he captained, pride for the crew he commanded, and pride for the country he served.

~~

Pearl stood at the A Deck forward railing, enjoying the feel of the wind whipping through her clothes.

The *Titanic* plowed through the waves, the knife-edge of the prow slicing through the surface. The ship had truly been designed by brilliant architects. There was hardly a bump of the ship from the waves, never a feel of the hum from the engines, nor a sense of being at sea at all. The only clue a passenger had of the fact that they were at sea came when one looked out at the ocean surrounding them.

The ship moved so effortlessly through the water, but the work of operating the ship was far from effortless. Everything had to work together in perfect harmony to make it possible. Stokers in the boiler rooms throwing coal into the fire, engineers in the engine rooms operating the turbines and pistons in just the right way to turn the exact propellers they needed, the stewards catering to every whim of the passengers to ensure a pleasant journey, the officers and captain commanding every crew member on the ship…Everyone on the ship had a purpose, adding their small part to the bigger picture.

Pearl closed her eyes and allowed the caress of the gentle breeze to ensnare her mind. She could imagine that if she let her hair down, it would whip about in the wind. She smiled as she opened her eyes again. Knowing it was about time to head down and take care of family business, she turned and headed for her cabin.

After changing from her first-class dress to her third-class attire, Pearl entered the third-class general room on C Deck and found a seat at one of the tables, watching the passengers around her as they conversed. She felt a hand on her shoulder and turned to find herself face-to-face with her great grandmother.

"Have I met you b'foor?" Constance asked in an Irish accent, frowning slightly.

Pearl turned completely to face her. "No, I just have one of those faces."

They stared into each other's eyes. It was as if they could both sense that they were related. Pearl noticed that Constance's eyes were blue; she definitely did not get her green eyes from her.

Pearl smiled up at her great grandmother, who held her infant son in her arms. Pearl gazed closely at the baby, recognizing him from pictures of Sean as a baby. It truly was him; it was all true.

"He's such a beautiful baby!" Pearl told Constance.

Constance looked down at the infant in her arms. "Thank you."

"What is his name?"

Constance looked up at Pearl. "Willyum."

Pearl smiled when she heard her grandfather's real name. William was a nice name in its own right, but he would always be Sean to her.

"That's a strong name," said Pearl. "It means protector."

Constance smiled. "It duz? Tha's wondurful." She looked down at her son, smiling. "It suits 'im."

"Wha' suits 'oo?" asked Lachlan as he strode up to the three of them. He also had an Irish accent.

Pearl also noticed that Lachlan had green eyes like her, and she let a small smile escape onto her face.

"Our son," Constance told him. "'Is name means protector."

Lachlan smiled, nodding. "O' course it duz." He leaned down, placing a hand on his son's small head. "This lit'ul guy is goin' t' be strong...jus' like 'is daddy."

Constance and Pearl laughed a little.

~~

Pearl left the general room, trying to free herself from the crowd. She had talked with her great grandparents for approximately an hour, exhausting her mental strength. Constance had requested that she accompany her husband, her son and herself to the stern for some air. Pearl had politely declined, saying she wanted to rest. Her family had mercifully let her disappear.

Now, Pearl headed for her cabin, looking for a respite. She lay down on her bunk, closing her eyes. She stretched her arms above her head, getting the kinks out of her muscles. After her elbows popped, she let her arms fall to the thin mattress with a sigh.

Pearl opened her eyes and glanced over at the digital watch strapped to the bed railing. It was four o'clock; dinner began in two hours.

Just enough time for a small nap, Pearl thought with a smile as she set the alarm on the watch and closed her eyes.

It felt as though she had just closed her eyes when the alarm went off in her ear. She switched it off and climbed to her feet, opening her door and heading into the corridor and up the staircase. She headed down the corridors of F Deck, entering the third-class dining saloon to see a fairly empty dining room. Dinner did not start for another twenty minutes. Pearl sat herself at the end of one of the tables, waiting patiently for the rest of the passengers to appear.

It did not take long for guests to accumulate at the tables, and before long, stewards began to bring out the first dishes. Tonight's menu consisted of tomato soup, corned beef and cabbage with potatoes, and a peaches and rice pudding. Overall, it was not that bad.

Pearl left the dining saloon at eight o'clock, returning to her room to write in her journal and retiring shortly thereafter.

11

April the Twelfth

Pearl lost her grip and began slipping down the wooden surface, fumbling her arms around for something to grab onto. A hand came out of nowhere, grasping onto her arm. She looked up at her savior.

"I got you!" Sam told her as he held onto the stern railing with his other hand. "Just hold onto me! I won't let you go!"

Pearl raised her other arm and grasped onto his arm. Sam pulled her towards him, latching her hand onto the railing next to him. Pearl pulled herself to the cold metal as Sam circled an arm around her.

"It'll be okay," Sam told her. "I'm here. You'll be okay. I promise."

"I'm scared, Sam," Pearl confided.

"I know, Pearl," Sam consoled her. "I know. But I'm here with you."

Pearl and Sam watched as the passengers around them scrambled across the deck away from the pull of the ocean. A loud sound rang out, almost as though a great metal door had slammed shut.

Pearl and Sam tightened their grip as the massive ship fell underneath them. Pearl's stomach shot up into her throat as she dropped with the ship. The ship abruptly stopped underneath them. As they slammed onto the deck, the stern rocked on the waves in the water.

"Come on!" yelled Sam. "We have to go!"

He swung his leg over the railing as the stern tilted. Once on the outside of the railing, he grabbed onto Pearl's arm and pulled her over with him. They lay on the white metal as the stern froze in the air and began sinking.

"Hold on!" Sam warned as they were plunged into the icy water.

The suction pulled them apart and deeper, showing no mercy.

Pearl inhaled deeply as she jack-knifed up in her bed, shaking. She glanced around at the simple cabin she had woken up in. The morning sun shone into the room slightly from the porthole high in the wall of her third-class room.

Pearl breathed a sigh of relief. She was safe.

Well, as safe as you can be on the Titanic…

Pearl climbed out of bed, going about her morning routine of bathing, dressing and heading to the first-class dining saloon for breakfast, after which she would head to the Turkish baths.

~~

117

J. Bruce Ismay shook Captain Smith's hand as he walked onto the bridge, beaming proudly at the esteemed captain.

"E.J.," greeted Ismay. "Everything going splendid, I see."

"Yes," concurred Smith. "Absolutely splendid."

"Excellent, excellent," grinned Ismay. "How has she been fairing?"

"The roster had the crossing at three hundred and sixty-five miles so far this morning," Smith informed him. "We shall see how many we have made in a day when the time has come."

Ismay frowned. "Three hundred and sixty-five? Is that all?"

"Mr. Ismay, we had only begun the voyage the day previously," Smith told him. "We stopped at Queenstown and did not leave until 1:30. Naturally, the first day would only consist of a few hundred miles."

"Of course, of course," said Ismay, feeling reassured about the mileage. "Carry on, then."

"We will, Mr. Ismay," said Smith. "Now, if you wouldn't mind, I need to get back to commanding my ship."

"Yes, yes," agreed Ismay. "All the best."

Ismay left the bridge, leaving Smith to his crew. Smith watched him leave, wondering how much longer he would have to put up with the steamship millionaire.

~~

Pearl walked down the A Deck promenade after taking a swim in the Turkish baths, watching the people around her. She spotted an older couple just ahead, lounging in two deck chairs. The man had a full mustache and gray hair. The woman had dark brown hair and a small, shrewd face.

Pearl approached them. "Sir Duff Gordon."

Sir Cosmo Duff Gordon looked up at Pearl and gracefully stood to greet her. "Yes, madam."

"Such an honor to meet you. I am Pearl Liberti."

"Pleasure to meet you, Miss Liberti," said Sir Duff Gordon. He motioned his hand towards his wife, who had stood to greet Pearl. "This is my wife Lucy."

"How do you do?" asked Pearl.

"Splendid," declared Lady Duff Gordon.

"How is your fashion business fairing?" inquired Pearl.

"Oh, couldn't be better," replied Lady Duff Gordon.

Pearl turned to Sir Duff Gordon. "I heard the other day that you had represented Great Britain in the 1908 Olympics."

Sir Duff Gordon smiled and chuckled. "Yes, I did."

"What was your specialty?" asked Pearl.

"I was a fencer," answered Sir Duff Gordon.

"That is certainly interesting," said Pearl. "Well, I wish you many successful years to come."

"To you, as well," expressed Sir Duff Gordon.

Pearl turned, heading on her way down the deck. She soon came upon an older man with a wild, white beard.

"Mr. Stead," Pearl greeted. "Hello, my name is Pearl Liberti."

"Hello, Miss Liberti," said William Thomas Stead. "I am surprised you know who I am."

"I recognized you from a picture in the paper," Pearl told him. "I've read your work."

"Well, thank you," said Stead. "It's always nice to hear someone appreciates my work."

W.T. Stead was a British journalist and spiritualist who wrote a novel, titled *From the Old World to the New*, in 1892. His book told the story of a ship striking an iceberg in the North Atlantic and sinking. The survivors were picked up by the *Majestic*, which was captained by E.J. Smith.

Another coincidental novel was *Futility*, written by Morgan Robertson. The premise involved a supposedly unsinkable British liner called the *Titan*. As it was attempting a record crossing from Southampton to New York in April, carrying two thousand passengers, the starboard hull was punctured by an iceberg. The *Titan* sank, leaving only thirteen survivors, due mainly to the shortage of lifeboats.

The similarity between the stories of the *Titan* and the *Titanic* is striking, and not merely because of their names. Both ships sailed their maiden voyage in April from Southampton to New York. Both carried around two thousand passengers. Both had triple-screw propellers. Both had a top speed of twenty-five knots. Both were over eight hundred feet in length. Both had a displacement around 66,000 tons. Both ships struck an iceberg on the starboard hull. Both sunk with a loss of life caused by a shortage of lifeboats. All of this is remarkably coincidental, especially considering the book was written fourteen years before the *Titanic* set sail.

Many instances like these presented themselves, both before and during the voyage. Many passengers and citizens had dreams or premonitions about the ship before she sailed. This caused a few passengers to change their plans. After all the public's claims that the ship was "unsinkable," they would be stunned to discover it had sunk in the early hours of Monday morning.

"It's odd, isn't it?" asked Stead.

Pearl turned her attention back to the journalist. "What is odd?"

"Our captain…Edward John Smith," said Stead. "E.J. That was the name of a captain in one of my stories."

"You don't say," smiled Pearl.

"What an amazing coincidence," said Stead. "Well, I must be off. I promised Colonel Gracie a game in the squash court. Have a pleasant day."

"You also," said Pearl.

Pearl set off down A Deck, intent on mingling with the first-class passengers.

~~

Pearl left the first-class dining saloon, having just finished lunch at 2:30. She headed up to B Deck, walking down the corridor. She looked around to make sure no one stood in the corridor before she opened the door to a first-class parlor suite, entering to take a look around. As she closed the door, she turned the camera in her glasses on.

The sitting room held a couple chairs and couches for reclining on top of an ornate rug. A fireplace stood in the wall to the right, framed by a marble mantle. The walnut walls adorned with gold leafing enclosed the room, stretching up to a white ceiling. A door in the left wall led to a private drawing room. Pearl headed through the drawing room, spotting the door ahead of her.

Pearl walked through the door to the bedroom. On the right side of the room sat a small desk with a chair in front of it. A small lamp stood on the walnut desktop. The chair had a walnut frame with a gold seat and back cushions. The back was shaped as a circle, separated from the seat by two posts of wood that held it up. The armrests had a small gold cushion on the top of them in the middle of the wood.

A reclining couch sat directly across the room against the wall opposite the door. This also had a walnut frame and gold upholstery. The ends of the recliner curled away from the center into the air. The back of the couch curved from the right side of the couch to the middle of the seat cushion.

A four-poster bed stood on the left side of the room. It was built into the corner of the room, so it really was more of a three-poster. The twin-sized bed supported the mattress in an oak frame. A dull green, striped, built-in bed skirt hung from the wooden frame, touching the forest green carpet.

The scarlet bed covers blended oddly with the olive green curtains, which were drawn back to the oak posts and held in place by gold tassels. Three layers of pillows lay at the head of the bed. The bottom layer consisted of one scarlet pillow. The next layer had two pillows side-by-side, striped scarlet and gold. The final pillow was a small round gold one with tassels on each end.

At the foot of the bed, a railing rose to chest-height. A curved arch in the wood connected each post in the railing.

Following the bed posts up to the ceiling, Pearl saw that oak beams crisscrossed the ceiling, creating white recessed squares above her.

The walls held remarkable detail. The top half had been decorated with scarlet and gold wallpaper. From shoulder-height down, oak paneling ran to the floor. On each wall, a brass scone with a glass lamp cover hung, supporting two light bulbs. One scone even hung over the head of the bed. Set into the wall at the foot of the bed was a door to the corridor.

Oh, man... Pearl thought with longing. *I wish I was staying in a first-class suite.*

Pearl heard the door handle of the sitting room being turned, so she made a hasty exit through the door in the bedroom to the corridor. Pearl quietly closed the bedroom door, looking down the corridor to see an elderly couple just entering the sitting room down the hall.

That was a close call, Pearl thought.

She breathed out a sigh of relief as she headed down the corridor, entering the area of the grand staircase and turning off the glasses.

As she headed up the stairs towards the Boat Deck, someone brushed against her shoulder. Pearl looked at the middle-aged Mexican man who had lightly bumped her.

"Terribly sorry, miss," he told her.

"Oh, it's fine," said Pearl.

The man held his hand out. "Manuel Uruchurtu."

Pearl shook his hand. "Pearl Liberti."

She was struggling to recall which passenger he was, and she almost had it.

"Again, terribly sorry," said Manuel. "You have a pleasant evening."

"Thank you," said Pearl.

As the man walked into the crowd, Pearl finally remembered.

Manuel Uruchurtu had been exiled to France because he had too much money. Now, he had arranged a return to Mexico to bring his wife with him to Paris. Unfortunately, he would not survive.

There were many who had plans, just as Manuel did. And just like Manuel, the plans had been interrupted by the *Titanic*'s own catastrophic plans. Honeymoons, business trips, emigrations, weddings...all had either been put on hold or terminated completely.

Pearl turned back towards the staircase, heading up to the Boat Deck. She emerged in the sunshine, basking in the warmth. It felt much more comfortable on decks than it did yesterday. Of course, it was still April in the North Atlantic, but at least the sun was warming the decks to the point where the cloak was no longer needed. She had stowed the cloak under the staircase in the aft well deck that led to B Deck.

Pearl headed for the enclosed top portion of the first-class lounge, sitting down in one of the deck chairs positioned there. She watched people walk past her, enjoying the view of the ocean around them. They had not a care in the world, nor a dread of things to come.

Pearl glanced down at her pocket watch, hearing the faint ticking as the second hand moved around the watch face. It signaled the time that was flying past, unable to be held captive for even a moment. If only time could stand still and the crowd onboard could enjoy this voyage for eternity. Nevertheless, the seconds ticked by, pushing the ship and its passengers towards their destiny.

~~

Pearl walked down the grand staircase, descending to D Deck. It was six o'clock; time to eat dinner. Pearl entered the D Deck Reception Room, mingling among the passenger elite. She said hello to many passengers she had already met and introduced herself to several more passengers.

Making her way into the dining room, she seated herself at one of the smaller tables off to the side.

"Hello, dear," a voice said from her right.

Pearl turned and saw Margaret Brown standing at her shoulder.

"Hello, Margaret," Pearl greeted.

"Is anyone sitting with you?" asked Margaret.

"Not at all," Pearl told her. "You're welcome to join me."

"I think I will," said Margaret. She sat down across from her at the table. "Pleasant evening, isn't it?"

"Oh, yes," agreed Pearl. "It's a lovely voyage."

"Lovely indeed," said Margaret.

A few minutes later, they were joined by a woman and her daughter.

"Evening, ladies," said the woman. "May we join you?"

"You may," said Margaret with a smile. "The name is Margaret Brown."

"Pearl Liberti," Pearl introduced herself as the two newcomers took seats at the table.

"Ida Hippach," greeted the woman. "This is my daughter Jean."

"Nice to meet the two of you," said Margaret. "Are you returning home or vacationing?"

"We were vacationing in Europe," Ida informed them. "We are returning to our home in Chicago, Illinois."

"Oh, an American woman," said Margaret. "As am I. I live in Denver, Colorado. I toured Europe and Africa after visiting my daughter. She decided to stay behind in France. It is unfortunate that she missed the occasion to travel with me on the *Titanic*." Margaret looked across the table at Pearl. "Where do you hail from, Pearl?"

"I also live in Chicago," Pearl told them. "I had been vacationing in Europe also."

"What a coincidence," said Margaret.

With that declaration, the four women leapt into a delightful conversation as the food arrived.

~~

"It was a Monday, a day like any other day! I left a small town for the apple in decay! It was my destiny! It's what we needed to do! They were telling me! I'm telling you!"

126

Pearl sat on a wooden bench on the fantail after the first-class dinner, leaning back and gazing at the stars. She was quietly singing another favorite song: Foreigner's "Long, Long Way from Home."

"I was inside, looking outside!" Pearl sang. *"The millions of faces, but still I'm alone! Waiting, hours of waiting, paying a penance! I was longing for home!"*

Pearl was surprised at how bright the stars twinkled at her. She lived in the city and had not glimpsed the stars since she was a teenager. Being in this simpler time…being out in the middle of the ocean…she could see them so clearly.

"I'm looking out for the two of us!" Pearl sang. *"I hope we'll be here when they're through with us! Monday! Sad, sad Monday! She's waiting for me, but I'm a long, long way from home!"*

Pearl was a long, long way from home in this time and place. Likewise, the passengers on this ship with her were also far from their homes, traveling to a world completely unknown to them. She turned her attention back to the stars above her.

Pearl had never really pictured herself as a stargazer. They all looked so beautiful, generating inspiration in the mind. Each pinpoint of light told its own story, beaming its light across galaxies and solar systems.

Pearl looked over at the stern railing and realized this was the night in the movie that Rose tried to jump. Pearl smiled as she walked over to the stern railing and gazed down at the torrent caused by the propellers.

That would be quite a drop, thought Pearl.

She looked out at the stars, thinking about the days to come.

Pearl only had two days left on the ship; everything was moving too fast. It seemed as though it were only a minute ago that she was standing on that platform in the time lab. Her journey was already halfway completed. She had thought she had all the time in the world to enjoy the experience, but now the end of the voyage was drawing to a close.

Pearl began thinking of her friends back home: Katrina, Kyle, Rose, Chris, Mary, Connor and Sam. She wondered what they were doing at that moment while she was on this ship, staring at the stars.

Pearl shook her head, thinking, *Of course they're not doing anything, you idiot.*

The pendant would bring her back within ten seconds of the moment she had left. They would have time for nothing more than breathing and blinking.

Pearl glanced at her watch, seeing that it was ten o'clock.

No wonder no one is up here, Pearl thought.

She turned and headed down to her room for the night.

12

Ghosts Among Us

"Come on, Sam!" yelled Pearl. "We have to hurry! It's already 11:30!"

Sam followed Pearl as they dashed through the first-class corridors.

They burst into the grand staircase, tearing through the door to the promenade and startling the other passengers. They sped forward down the A Deck promenade, slamming to a stop at the railing. They could not see the monster ahead of them in the darkness, but they knew it was there, just waiting for them.

Pearl glanced up at the Boat Deck two decks above them, spotting First Officer Murdoch at the railing.

"Murdoch!" Pearl screamed at the top of her voice.

Murdoch startled and began looking around for the source of the voice.

"Down here!" Pearl yelled.

Murdoch glanced down at Pearl, a frown on his face.

"Iceberg!" Pearl called, pointing a finger at the bow.

Murdoch gazed into the darkness ahead, narrowing his eyes. Sure enough, a moment later he made out a dark shape ahead of the ship. Pearl watched as he tore away from the railing.

"Hard-a-starboard!"

Pearl heard the telegraphs spin on the bridge. About two minutes later, Pearl watched the bow head to the left of the iceberg, missing the leviathan by a few dozen feet.

"Hard-a-port!"

The liner then made a slow turn towards the right, the stern avoiding a hit. Pearl smiled as the Titanic *sailed on, safe and whole.*

Murdoch glanced down at her, a smile on his face. "Thank you, miss."

Pearl opened her eyes to a gentle hum as the engines moved the liner across the Atlantic. She closed her eyes once more, wishing beyond hope that she could make her dream a reality.

Pearl finally pulled herself out of her bed, dressing and heading up for breakfast in the third-class dining saloon. Sitting down at one of the tables, she waited for the stewards to bring the food out.

Breakfast seemed to consist of more portions than her dinner on Thursday the eleventh. She had porridge with milk—although, she skipped the milk due to her lactose intolerance—kippers and onions, baked potatoes, fresh bread and butter, marmalade and tea. Concluding her breakfast at 9:30, she headed back down to her cabin to finish washing up and dressing.

Pearl climbed the stairs to C Deck, entering the general room with her journal to sit at one of the tables and meet with passengers.

Before long, four men sat down not far from her at the table. The youngest of the men glanced up and spotted Pearl writing in her journal.

"Writing a book?" he asked with a British accent.

Pearl smiled as she looked up at him. "Just writing in my journal."

"Oh," said the man. "Looks interesting."

Pearl laughed.

"Joseph Davies," the man introduced himself.

Pearl smiled. "Pearl Liberti."

Now that Pearl had the youngest man's name, she knew who the other three were. The oldest man was James Lester, and the other two were Alfred J. Davies and John S. Davies. Alfred, John and Joseph were brothers, and James was their uncle. All four were traveling to Michigan, where they had been offered jobs. Alfred had been married two days prior to the voyage, and his wife had stayed behind in England to follow at a later date. Unfortunately, the two newlyweds would never see each other again. All four men would go down with the ship.

"Well, I'll not bother you a moment longer," said Joseph.

Pearl smiled. "Nice to meet you."

"You also," said Joseph, turning back to his brothers.

Pearl looked up at a family of four seated a few tables down from her position. She recognized the family from a popular photograph: it was the Dean family.

Bertram Dean and his wife Eva Dean were traveling with their one-year-old son Bertram and nine-week-old daughter Elizabeth, most commonly known as Millvina. All of the family besides the husband survived, naming Millvina as the youngest survivor of the disaster. As of 2005, Millvina Dean was among one of the three survivors still alive. Well, four, including Pearl's grandfather.

Pearl knew the stories of so many of the passengers around her, having studied the tales and legends of the *Titanic* for years. Her extensive knowledge of the voyage surprised her sometimes, how the human mind can capture and recall so much information.

After spending an hour in the general room, Pearl gathered her things and headed in the direction of the stern to take in the morning air. It was a pleasant day, the sun shining down on the decks. Pearl took a seat in one of the deck chairs, basking in the warmth. She closed her eyes, letting the ship's movements lull her into a restful peace.

"Miss?"

Pearl opened her eyes to see a sailor standing next to her chair.

"Yes?" Pearl asked.

"I thought you might want to go to lunch," the sailor told her.

"Lunch?" Pearl asked, taking a look around. She noticed that the shadows on the deck had changed direction slightly since she had last seen them. "What time is it?"

"One o'clock, miss," the sailor replied.

"Oh, yes, thank you," said Pearl.

The sailor went about his duty as Pearl climbed to her feet.

Returning from the fantail, Pearl descended to F Deck to eat lunch in the third-class dining saloon. She finished her lunch around two o'clock, heading to her cabin to write in her journal and relax before changing into her first-class attire to head to the D Deck Reception Room.

~~

Captain Edward John Smith glanced around at the men and women enjoying their tea and caviar in the Reception Room.

"So, you've decided to not light all of the boilers?" J. Bruce Ismay questioned.

Smith looked back over at Ismay, who sat adjacent to him at the table.

"Of course not," Smith told him. "We are making excellent time. She is performing beautifully."

"Yes, yes, of course she is," dismissed Ismay. "But imagine the stories when we show them just how fast the *Titanic* can go."

"Mr. Ismay..." began Smith. "This is the maiden voyage of the *Titanic*. She needs to be properly run-in. I would prefer not to push the engines before they have had the chance to get used to working."

"Of course, of course," said Ismay. "But imagine: *Titanic* arriving before the reporters can turn out in the harbor."

"Mr. Ismay," said Smith, his voice taking on a more authoritative tone. "I hope you know that the *Titanic* cannot win the Blue Riband. The record is twenty-six knots with the *Mauretania*. *Titanic* is only capable of reaching twenty-four knots."

"Of course I know this," Ismay brushed off. "You of all people should know that I despise the steamer race. My goal is not to achieve the Blue Riband. But...think of how this would look as your final crossing. We will beat the *Olympic* and get into New York on Tuesday. The great Edward John Smith goes out with a bang."

Smith looked down at the table, contemplating.

What harm could it do? Smith reasoned. *I have complete trust in my crew.*

Smith looked up at Ismay, nodding his consent.

Ismay smiled. "Good. It's settled."

Smith excused himself to go inform his crew, walking past a table where a red-headed woman sat alone.

Pearl looked up at Smith and back at Ismay. *I knew it.*

Captain Smith's decision had been made in haste and under peer pressure. Of course, he saw that the weather had been clear throughout the voyage and his crew had been expertly trained. He reasoned that any danger would be seen long in advance and would be avoided proficiently. What he did not see was that his decision had just secured the future of everyone onboard.

Pearl gravely climbed to her feet and made her way out of the Reception Room, heading back to her cabin to change back into her third-class dress and relax in her cabin.

As she lay on her bed, she stared at the ceiling, thinking about the coming night. The iceberg would be colliding in less than thirty-six hours, creating history and changing the lives of everyone onboard. Pearl knew that she could not interfere, but her heart wrenched at the thought of leaving these people to their fate.

On the one hand, she could save the passengers and let them go about their lives. No one would have to die, and no one would have to mourn their lost ones.

On the other hand, she knew she had to let history play out the way it was meant to, but could she live with herself if she did so? If you knew what the future held and did nothing to stop it...was that the same as murder?

~~

After dinner had finished at eight o'clock, the steerage passengers had traveled to the C Deck general room to celebrate the voyage. The ship's rule, although more an encouraged rule than enforced, was that the third-class should retire to their cabins at ten o'clock every night. This gave the people two hours to enjoy themselves before heading to sleep.

Pearl sat in the general room, watching the steerage passengers enjoy their party. It was a pleasant change of pace from first-class. Sure, first-class was elegant and opulent, but third-class was entertaining. There were no class rules and etiquette here. People were allowed to act however they wanted here, with no need to impress anyone.

Pearl thought that if she had lived in this time, she would want to be of the steerage class. Sure, they may not have money or good jobs or a promising future...but at least they were happy.

Young couples danced vigorously to the upbeat Irish music being played by a small band in the corner. Little children jumped around the room, caught up in the high spirits of the moment. The benches and chairs had been drawn up against the walls around the room to make a space for dancing. Many passengers sat on the benches and chairs, happily discussing everything under the sun.

The only irritant was the cigarette smoke accumulating in the air. The smell stung Pearl's nostrils and caused her eyes to water.

A young man burst out of the crowd, spinning and jumping every which way. The people cheered and clapped as he smiled goofily, soaking up the attention. He dazedly began spinning faster, the beer obviously in his bloodstream aiding his uninhibited state. His inebriated body finally grew unbalanced, and he collapsed to the floor with a great crash. The crowd laughed and applauded the man as someone helped him to his feet.

Pearl's gaze swept the crowd, landing on the gates that lingered open in the doorway. The smile slowly faded from Pearl's face as she stared at the black metal. In twenty-four hours, those gates would close, never to be opened again. Many of the people in this room with her would be trapped below decks by those very gates.

A hand landed on her shoulder, and Pearl looked at the red-headed woman next to her. The woman narrowed her eyes, looking concerned.

"Are you a'right?" asked the woman in a kind, deep Irish voice. "You look like you've seena ghos'."

I'm looking at one right now, Pearl thought.

Pearl smiled. "I'm just a bit tired, I suppose. I'll be fine."

The woman's face lit up with a smile. "O' course. I'm a bit tired meself. It mus' be goin' 'round."

136

"Must be," said Pearl, turning back to the party.

"In that case, I think I will turn in far the nigh'," said the woman, getting to her feet. "Les see if I can' get a couple extra hars o' sleep."

"Good night," Pearl told her.

"Good nigh'," the woman said with a small wave. "Is shoor to be a peaceful 'un."

She turned and began heading around the crowd.

"Enjoy it while it lasts," Pearl whispered under her breath.

She climbed to her feet and set off for her cabin, knowing she should get some extra sleep for tomorrow night.

~~

Pearl clung onto Sam as he tried to usher her towards the last lifeboat.

"No, I won't go without you!" Pearl told him.

"You have to," Sam told her. "We'll see each other again someday."

"No, I won't leave you!" Pearl exclaimed as she wrapped her arms tighter around Sam's neck. "If you die, I die."

"Pearl, please," Sam begged. "I need to know that you'll be okay. As long as you're safe, I'll always be with you."

Pearl began crying as Sam took her face in his hands.

"Please go," Sam pleaded with her. "I'll be okay."

Pearl gripped him tight, pulling him in for a kiss.

"Women and children only!"

Lightoller's cry broke their passionate goodbye, and Sam brought her to the edge of the deck. Lightoller shot a hand out, gripping Pearl's arm to help her over the three-inch gap in between the boat and the ship. A sailor helped her into the boat as Sam leaned forward.

"I love you," Sam told her.

Pearl smiled sadly, a tear falling down her face. "I love you."

"Lower away!" Lightoller commanded.

A jolt ran through the loaded boat as the sailors on the Boat Deck began easing rope through the wenches and davits. The boat slowly lowered inch by inch towards the water.

Pearl gazed up at Sam, who stood at the railing and watched her depart the doomed ship. Her vision blurred as her eyes filled with tears. As the boat hit the water, the cables attached to the funnel snapped, sending the large funnel onto the crowded deck where Sam stood.

"No!" Pearl cried as she jolted up in bed.

She took in the cabin around her with its calm décor. She clasped the locket around her neck, where the picture of her and Sam resided.

It's okay, Pearl, she reminded herself. *He's safe in 2005.*

Pearl sighed in relief until she realized what today's date was: April 14, 1912.

Titanic's last day.

13

Sunday Tour

As the first-class passengers assembled in the dining chairs in front of the altar, Captain Smith stepped up to the pulpit. The green leather chairs had been taken from their usual places at the tables and assembled in small rows at the forward section of the dining saloon.

In front of the makeshift pews stood an altar covered with a white cloth. A small vase of white flowers sat upon the altar, accompanied by a cross and a folded British flag. The pulpit stood erect behind the altar, and behind the pulpit sat the piano.

Captain Smith removed his white peaked cap and placed it on the pulpit. Everyone quieted down and gazed up at their captain.

"Good morning, ladies and gentlemen," Captain Smith pronounced with a smile. "Thank you for joining us on this Sunday morning. I will now lead the mass in a prayer for those at sea. Please bow your heads."

Pearl bowed her head along with the others as Smith recited his prayer.

"Our Father in heaven, we thank you for this day and for our blessed journey. We pray that you watch over those at sea and keep them from harm during their travels. Above all, we ask that you keep them in your thoughts and heart from this day forth. Amen."

"Amen," the assembly recited.

Pearl looked up at the Captain, who picked up his program and nodded at the man at the piano. The passengers rose from their chairs to begin the worship ceremony. The piano struck up an eerily familiar hymn. Pearl listened to the words as they were sung by her and the other passengers.

"Eternal Father, strong to save, whose arm hath bound the restless wave; who bidst the mighty ocean deep, its own appointed limits keep. Oh, hear us when we cry to Thee, for those in peril on the sea."

What the other passengers did not realize was that they had just said a prayer for themselves. For, indeed, in thirteen hours, every one of them would be "in peril on the sea." And there was nothing Pearl could do to stop it. None of the dreams she had been having the past four nights would come true, but over two thousand people would be facing that exact same terror tonight.

A tear slipped from Pearl's eye and trailed down her cheek. She hastily wiped it away and composed herself.

"Are you all right, miss?" a gentleman next to her asked.

Pearl looked at him, but did not recognize him. Donning the presumption of female foolishness, Pearl clasped a hand to her heart.

"Oh, it's just that this song is so beautiful!" Pearl told the man.

The man turned his head back to his program, mumbling something that sounded suspiciously like, "Women."

~~

Pearl offered her program to the steward at the dining saloon doors, spotting a familiar face at the base of the grand staircase. Pearl approached him, smiling.

"Mr. Andrews," greeted Pearl.

Thomas Andrews smiled and accepted her hand, kissing the fingers. "Good morning, Miss Liberti. Ready for the tour, I see."

"Oh, yes," Pearl told him. "I am very gracious to you for allowing me to accompany you."

"Oh, it's no trouble," Andrews assured her. He glanced down at her empty hands. "Don't you need a paper and pen?"

"Oh, I have a very good memory," Pearl explained.

In reality, she was recording this whole thing with her glasses.

"Well, then, shall we begin?" Andrews asked, extending his elbow.

Pearl looped her arm through his, and they started off. Andrews escorted Pearl up through the decks and onto the bridge, showing her through the entryway.

"This, madam, is the bridge," said Andrews. "This is where the crew oversees the workings of the ship. From here, they can steer, plot our course and radio to various parts of the ship."

The captain entered the bridge, and Andrews led Pearl over to him.

"Ah, Captain Smith," greeted Andrews. "I'd like you t' meet Pearl Liberti. She is writing a newspaper article on the ship."

"Pleasure to meet you, Miss Liberti," smiled Smith, extending a hand.

Pearl smiled and shook his hand. "And to you as well, Captain."

"Captain," came a voice behind Smith.

The small group turned to see a young man with a slip of paper in his hand. He wore black pants, a white long-sleeved shirt, black tie and black vest.

"Yes, Bride?" asked Captain Smith.

The young man, Second Wireless Operator Harold Bride, held the small paper up. "I have an ice warning from the *Noordam*. Their report correlates with the position the *Caronia* gave us."

Smith nodded as he accepted the piece of paper. "Thank you, Mr. Bride."

Bride nodded and headed back to the Marconi Room.

Chief Officer Henry Wilde walked over, having heard the report. "Orders, sir?"

Smith contemplated his choices for a moment before answering. "Maintain speed and heading, Mr. Wilde."

Wilde nodded. "Yes, sir."

Pearl screamed inside her head for someone to challenge the captain. The position of reported ice—42° North, 49° to 51° West— lay directly in their path. Surely, someone should suggest adjusting their heading further south. However, no one had authority over the captain, so, of course, no one challenged him. They had no reason to do so.

Edward John Smith was one of the most experienced captains on the seven seas; he was even referred to as the Millionaire's Captain.

Captain Smith felt no need for intervention because he saw no danger for them. Icebergs usually never traveled this far south. He probably thought they would melt in the warm current and spring sun by the time the *Titanic* reached them.

The *Titanic* was considered the safest ship in operation—its own lifeboat. Watertight bulkheads divided the lower compartments all the way to E Deck. The ship had the new third screw propeller, increasing its efficiency in speed and turning. Two lookouts stood in the crow's nest around the clock, keeping a look out for possible perils. They had designed the ship to deal with any amount of problems: a puncture in two or more compartments, a head-on collision that filled the front four compartments…

No one ever foresaw what happened that night. No one, least of all the captain, expected danger to come their way.

Smith noticed the forlorn look on Pearl's face. "Not to worry. We keep a sharp eye out for the bergs. We'll have plenty of notice if we see one."

Pearl tried to smile and nod. "Certainly."

Andrews looked at her. "You wanted t' see the Marconi Room, correct?"

"Yes, please," said Pearl.

The two of them bade the captain farewell and made their way through the wheelhouse and to the Marconi Room.

Harold Bride stood at a desk, sorting through small papers. A second young man, First Wireless Operator Jack Phillips, sat at the wireless desk, tapping away on the radio. Phillips wore the same attire as Bride, although he also had a headset on his head.

Pearl noted a faint whiff of ozone in the room, emitting from the radio.

Andrews stood at the doorway with Pearl. "This is the Marconi Room. We use the Continental Morse Code t' send messages t' other ships and t' stations on land. The new Marconi radio can transmit up t' twelve hundred miles in fair weather."

Pearl stood staring at the machine that, in twelve hours' time, would be the saving grace of the seven hundred survivors.

"Ready t' proceed?" asked Andrews.

Pearl nodded. "Yes, please."

Andrews escorted Pearl down to A Deck and around the staircase to the elevators. As Pearl rounded the corner, she stopped suddenly, staring down the corridor.

"Everything all right, miss?" Andrews asked.

Pearl diverted her attention back towards Andrews. "Um…" Pearl looked back down the corridor, narrowing her eyes in confusion. "Yes." She looked up at Andrews. "Yes, I'm fine."

As Andrews escorted Pearl into one of the elevators, Pearl thought about what she had just seen. She could have sworn she saw her friend Mary Gemini down the hall, which was impossible. None of the others were traveling here; it was only Pearl.

She had been seeing her friends a couple times in the faces of the other passengers. She was obviously home-sick and imagining her friends being there with her. The mirage was probably some bizarre answer to the question she had been asking herself the past day, as though she were hoping for someone to help her decide what to do.

Pearl and Andrews descended to E Deck and headed through the corridors until they came to a staircase that headed down to G Deck.

"I apologize for the distance we have t' travel, miss," said Andrews. "There is no staircase that heads directly t' the engine room. Not many people journey this far into the bowels of the ship except for the crew."

"Oh, it's perfectly fine," Pearl assured him. "It's interesting getting to see the workings of the ship."

Andrews led her down the corridor to another staircase that led down to the Orlop Deck. They approached a doorway in the white wall. Andrews held the door for Pearl, granting her entrance into the engine room.

"And this is the engine room," Andrews told her. "It houses two reciprocating engines, each of which powers a propeller shaft on either side of the stern."

Pearl looked around at the humungous room, as tall as a three-story house. She was standing on the Chief Engineer's platform. In front of her, massive towers rose to the ceiling, chugging along as they pushed the ship. The pistons turned in their shafts, creating a thumping that resounded in the confines of the engine room. The engines acted as the life and heart of the ship, the pumping of the pistons the pulse of the ship.

Catwalks wound themselves among the engines high above them. Engineers moved along the catwalks and platforms, checking and rechecking the performance of the engines. Steam issued from the pipes in the floor. A gear sat at the foot of both rows of reciprocating engines, turning a shaft that ran the length of the room and led to a propeller at the stern.

"Behind us is the turbine engine room," Andrews explained. "It runs on the used steam from the main engines, turning the central screw propeller. This propeller can only turn in one direction, thereby providing our forward propulsion."

"Then how does the ship turn or reverse direction?" Pearl asked, playing the part of the studious reporter she was supposed to be.

"That is the job of the smaller propellers on either side of the central shaft," Andrews illustrated, pointing out the shafts in the room in front of them. "They can turn in either direction. When we need to turn, we power one down. This way, only one side of the ship is moving, and the ship will turn."

Pearl took one last look at the engine room.

"Ready, miss?" Andrews inquired.

Pearl nodded. "Yes."

~~

Pearl approached the railing of the Forecastle Deck in front of her, reaching her hands out. She clasped onto the metal, looking down at the water in front of her. It was open ocean as far as she could see. She looked down at the prow as it slid through the waves, water spraying up along the sides and fanning out from the ship in waves.

Standing at the front of this powerful giant as it steamed through the ocean, Pearl could not imagine a loftier moment. It was easy to understand the feelings of the crew; their sense that nothing could bring them down. This vantage point on the ship certainly gave Pearl that feeling.

Pearl smiled as a secret desire popped into her head.

I've always wanted to do this, she thought.

Pearl pressed her body to the railing for support and lifted her arms into the air, holding them out to her sides. The shawl which was wrapped around her shoulders whipped out behind her under her arms, flapping in the wind. The ocean stretched out before her as she stood at the bow, arms outstretched. She closed her eyes, savoring the breeze on her face. She took a deep breath, catching the scent of water in the air, much like the smell after a rainstorm.

Pearl opened her eyes again, staring at the horizon in front of them. With just under twelve hours until impact, Pearl was becoming slightly anxious. Somewhere out there in front of them, the iceberg gradually drew closer.

"Madam?"

Pearl looked behind her to see Thomas Andrews on the metal grating by the railing next to her.

"It's just very beautiful," said Pearl. "She truly is the Ship of Dreams."

Andrews smiled. "That she is."

14

Final Tasks

After Andrews and Pearl concluded the tour and returned to A Deck, they accompanied each other to lunch.

Lunch was a wonderful affair—corned beef, vegetables, dumplings, fillets of brill, chicken á la Maryland, grilled mutton chops, mashed potatoes, custard pudding, apple meringue, roast beef, smoked sardines...

First-class passengers truly ate in the lap of luxury. Even as Pearl swallowed down mouthful after mouthful, she could not figure out what some of these dishes were.

Pearl exited the dining saloon at 2:30 and headed for the first-class lounge to grab a book from the mahogany bookcase and take it to the reading room.

It was rooms such as the lounge and reading room where passengers could truly forget the fact that they were in the middle of an ocean. The rooms held an air of class and elegance, giving one the impression that they were standing in the parlor of a Victorian house.

Pearl cracked her book open and began reading, trying to give herself a sense of calm as the afternoon consumed the precious little time they had left. Two hours later, Pearl decided to head down to her cabin and put on her last elegant dress of the voyage for dinner.

As she was dressing, Pearl looked up to see that it was fifteen minutes until six o'clock. The time while she had been getting ready had passed by so hastily. In fact, the entire voyage had passed by so hastily. It felt like a day ago she had enjoyed her first meal onboard. Now, she was getting ready to enjoy her last meal onboard.

Once dressed and composed, Pearl emerged into the corridor and headed up to the grand staircase, once again depositing her cloak behind the well deck staircase.

Entering the first-class dining saloon via the grand staircase, Pearl spotted Cecily Miles, Edith Rosenbaum and Malvina Cornell in the crowd. Cecily gave a small wave in her direction, and Pearl walked over to her new friend.

"Hello, Pearl, sweetheart," said Cecily. "How are you this evening?"

"Excellent," said Pearl with a thin smile.

Cecily saw right through her act. "What is really bothering you?"

"Nothing," said Pearl, thinking quick and making up a story to cover her solemn attitude. "I just miss my husband, that's all."

"Oh," said Cecily, accepting her story. "Yes, of course. How long have you been away from him?"

It feels like a lifetime, although it was only four days ago, Pearl thought, but responded with, "Two weeks."

"Well, you will see him in three days," Cecily comforted her. "Join our table. We'll try to take your mind off of the whole thing."

"Thank you," said Pearl. "You're right. I **will** see him in three days."

Pearl sat down at the four-person table with the three women and conversed with them as dinner made its way to the dining tables.

Pearl glanced over to one of the larger tables and noticed the party the Wideners were throwing Captain Smith. He seemed to be enjoying the celebration, with no idea that, in almost six hours' time, he would be roused from his sleep by the disaster of all disasters.

The first-class passengers' last—and in some cases, final—meal included hors d'oevres, oysters, soup, salad, pâté, ice cream, fresh fruit and cheese. It was, without a doubt, one of the most elegant meals Pearl had the pleasure of partaking.

Excusing herself early in the pretense of retiring to her cabin to get some rest, Pearl ascended the grand staircase, wanting to catch the last sunset onboard this wonderful vessel.

Pearl walked up to the railing of the bulwark on forward starboard B Deck, placing her hands on the wood. She gazed at the sky in front of the ship, eyes wide to take it all in. She intended to absorb as much of this moment as she could. After all, it was *Titanic*'s final sunset.

"That was the last time Titanic *ever saw daylight."*[5]

---

[5] From James Cameron's *"Titanic."*

The sky looked like a painting that one would find hanging in the room of a high-class hotel. The clouds overhead covered the sky in a purple hue. The sun peeked out between the clouds and water directly ahead of them, casting an amber light over the ship and her occupants. At the edge of the clouds, pink shone from the sky, changing to orange and then yellow the closer to the water it got.

The sun slowly sank towards the horizon, proof that the world kept turning in spite of the tragedy that lay dead ahead. Pearl would be standing in this exact spot in four hours to watch the iceberg impale the *Titanic*.

Pearl turned and headed towards the first-class gymnasium, her final task for her free time on the voyage. She climbed the small staircase to A Deck and then the stairs of the grand staircase to the Boat Deck, walking through the door to the gymnasium.

This room seemed plainer than the rest of the ship; no treasures and luxury to impress the upper classes. This room had been intended purely for recreation.

The white plastered walls turned to oak paneling a few feet from the tile floor. A map of the world and a picture of the ship hung on a wood display wall on the right side of the room next to the big gymnasium clock.

A rowing machine sat in the middle of the room in front of the display wall. In front of the clock were two stationary bicycles that did not look all that different from twenty-first century cycling machines. Two benches sat across from the display wall next to the rowing machine.

At the far end of the room were the two electric horses. They looked like saddles next to machines in cages. In the other corner, a couple more apparatuses stood. Pearl was unsure as to what they were supposed to be.

Pearl did not really understand why Kyle and everyone wanted her to check out the gymnasium. It's not like anything exciting happened in here. In fact, this room seemed pretty mundane and ordinary; definitely not one of the better rooms aboard the ship. Perhaps Kyle just wanted her to cover as much of the ship as she could.

The gymnasium was abandoned at this time, the usual exercise time being the early morning. Everyone was currently in the dining rooms, finishing up dinner.

Pearl knew she should head back to the reading room and enjoy what little time she had left. After all, she had places to be in just two hours.

~~

Captain Smith walked onto the bridge, having just excused himself from the party the Wideners had thrown in the D Deck Saloon. Second Officer Charles Lightoller stood at the helm, overseeing the seamen on his watch.

Smith walked over to his second officer. "Report, Mr. Lightoller."

"Heading steady at South 86 degrees West," Lightoller reported. "Weather remains fair, hardly a breath of wind. Air temperature is thirty-three degrees Fahrenheit."

Smith smiled. "Excellent. We have good visibility."

"Yes, sir," said Lightoller. "I've warned the lookouts to keep a sharp eye. We expect to see ice before midnight."

"Good," commented Smith. He looked through the bridge windows to gaze at the calm ocean spread out in front of them. "I don't think I have ever seen the water so calm. No passenger getting seasick tonight."

Lightoller and Smith laughed quietly for a moment.

"It is a pity that the breeze has subsided," Lightoller remarked. "There's no wind to stir up the surf at the base of the bergs. It won't be as easy to spot the ice."

Smith nodded. "True. But even if the berg shows a blue side, we'll have sufficient warning."

"Agreed, sir," Lightoller assented.

Smith gazed up at the stars through the glass of the windows, becoming conscious of the fact that no moon shone in the sky above. The lookouts only had the light of the stars to work with. It significantly reduced the iceberg visibility, but Smith was not worried. The lookouts had been trained to spot trouble. They would give warning if they saw anything. Moreover, First Officer Murdoch had ordered the forward forecastle hatch closed and forward lights extinguished, preventing a glare for the lookouts. The ship would be fine.

"I'm off for the night," Smith informed Lightoller. "Wake me if it becomes at all doubtful. Maintain speed and heading."

"Very good, sir," Lightoller replied.

Smith left the bridge, retreating to his cabin with one final look forward past the bow. For some unfathomable reason, he could not shake the feeling that something lay out there in the distance, waiting for them.

~~

Pearl rested her hands on the gate in front of her. She stood at the entrance to the forward staircase on the starboard promenade of the Boat Deck, the gate in front of her separating the first-class and the officers.

Pearl could see two figures at the bulwark next to the bridge, discussing matters unknown. Maybe they were talking over how eerily calm the weather was. Maybe they were asking the other about the missing binoculars for the lookouts in the crow's nest. Perhaps it was simply a relay of incidents and instructions as they changed shifts.

One man headed towards the staircase by the bridge, probably making his rounds for the night. The other man placed his arms on the railing and gazed into the clear night.

It was ten o'clock, which meant that the figure at the railing was First Officer William Murdoch, having just relieved Second Officer Charles Lightoller from bridge duty. One of the things Lightoller had most likely disclosed to Murdoch was that they expected to see ice at any minute.

Pearl watched Murdoch as he slowly turned and entered the bridge to get out of the soft breeze created by the moving ship. By taking this shift, a tremendous burden had just been placed on Murdoch's shoulders. It would be him who gave the order to avoid the iceberg.

Pearl glanced once again at her watch. If it really was ten o'clock, that gave her an hour and a half to change into her special wetsuit, gather her belongings, tour the ship one last time, and make it to the railing of forward starboard B Deck.

Pearl turned and headed into the grand staircase, heading for C Deck and her hidden cloak.

~~

Second Wireless Operator Harold Bride accepted the paper notes from the steward, turning towards his co-operator Jack Phillips.

"Ten more messages," Bride told him. "At this rate, we won't be getting a break all night long."

"Tell me about it," Phillips told him, tapping out the passengers' messages to New York on the Morse code radio.

Phillips and Bride had been trafficking messages all day: passenger requests out and ice warnings in. The constant interruptions into their work were beginning to grow wearisome. Almost every ship on the Atlantic had radioed them about the ice—in some cases, multiple times. As if one warning wasn't sufficient enough to tell them.

"Oh, bugger!" Phillips exclaimed, yanking the headphones off of his head in shock at the loud signal.

He held one of the earpieces up to his ear, listening to an incoming message and translating the Morse code.

"Who is it this time?" asked Bride as he sorted through the messages that Phillips had yet to send.

"The *Californian*...again," Phillips responded. "He says they've been stopped by the ice."

"What do we care if they've been stopped by the ice?" complained Bride. "We're busy. Tell him to butt out."

Phillips turned back to the transmitter, tapping out a message. "Keep out! Shut up! You're jamming my signal. I'm working Cape Race."

Bride chuckled. "That ought to get his attention."

Phillips listened for a moment or so. "No reply. I think he's finally shut down."

"Thank God," sighed Bride, handing Phillips ten new messages. "Well, back to work."

"Oh, jolly good," Phillips muttered as he put the headphones on and set back to work sending the passenger messages.

Bride went back to sorting through new messages, thinking about the ignorant operator on the *Californian*. Bride shook his head in amazement. Really, there were more important things than ice warnings right now.

15

Iron and Ice

Pearl glanced at her watch...10:30; one hour and ten minutes until the collision.

Pearl reached the door and looked back at the bed and left-behind luggage. She glanced around the room that had been her home for the past five days. She sadly turned the light off and closed the door, lugging a bag behind her.

Pearl headed out into the third-class corridor, once again wrapped in a shawl to hide her first-class dress. She had changed into her special wetsuit before dressing herself in first-class attire. She was carrying her bag with a change of clothes, her spectacles, and anything else she needed to take back to the future. She knew she would not be coming back to the room anymore.

Pearl continued on until she found a deserted corridor. She pulled the glasses out, turned the camera on and pointed it at herself.

"April 14, 1912...10:30 p.m.," Pearl said. "I'm on G Deck getting ready for one last tour of the ship."

She turned the camera off and placed the glasses on her face. She found the stairway once more and climbed up towards C Deck. She entered the third-class general room to find a few passengers gathered there. Everyone else was in their rooms, sleeping.

Pearl went back through the doorway and found the door to the well deck, taking off her shawl and stowing it in her bag. She walked forward and headed down the portside first-class corridor towards the grand staircase. She started walking down the hall, but stopped and turned around, looking down the corridor.

In her mind's eye, she could see the scene from the movie when the water poured through this very corridor, knocking doors off their hinges and punching holes in the walls.

Pearl turned towards the grand staircase and made her way towards it. She reached the stairs and descended to the D Deck landing. When she arrived at C Deck, she placed a finger to the button on the side of the glasses' frame to turn the camera on so it could capture what she was seeing. She slowly made her way to D Deck, gazing at the candelabra on the post. She approached the dining room doors and entered. The dining room was deserted, the men in the smoking room and the women heading to bed.

As Pearl gazed at one of the bigger tables, she could see the images of Rose, Jack, Cal, Ruth and all the notorious elite passengers gathered there for dinner, laughing together. Her memory then flashed to a dining room filling up with water, the chairs and dishes floating away as they created an eerily beautiful clinking that sounded like wind chimes.

Pearl turned and entered the reception area. She recalled Jack escorting Rose as she introduced random passengers.

Pearl smiled as she made her way up the stairs towards A Deck. She reached the top and walked onto the promenade, heading aft towards the Palm Court. She entered the sliding glass doors and looked around at the café. She could see Cal, Rose, Ruth, Molly, Ismay and Andrews assembled for lunch. She hung around for a minute and headed for the grand staircase.

Pearl entered the parlor and looked toward the staircase. She could see Rose coming down the stairs towards Jack, and he kissed her hand.

As Pearl walked up the stairs to the Boat Deck, she watched as Jack ran down the stairs to reunite with Rose after she had jumped off the lifeboat.

Pearl reached the balcony and gazed at the glass dome. She could see it break under the weight of the water; the unrelenting ocean came pouring in, flooding the staircase and crushing its victims.

All these memories hit Pearl one after the other as she looked at her favorite haunt on the ship for the last time.

She descended the stairs to C Deck and approached the doors to the port-side corridor. As she reached the doorway to the corridor, she heard a shriek in her memory. She remembered Jack and Rose running from Lovejoy into the elevators, Rose giving Lovejoy the finger in an attempt to throw off the labels of society.

Pearl smiled as she turned back to the doorway and entered the corridor. She headed aft for the stern and arrived ten minutes later. She stood at the stern railing with her hands on the bars, looking down at the colossal wake created by the huge propellers.

Her memory flashed to the moment when Jack and Rose were introducing themselves, with Rose on the other side of the railing holding Jack's hand. The scene that quickly replaced it was one of chaos. Jack was on the other side of the railing now, and he was pulling Rose over as the stern tilted steeply. The ship came to a rest as Jack and Rose clung to each other, and the stern sunk slowly below the surface.

Pearl turned and headed back towards C Deck. She turned to her left and could see the spot where Father Thomas Byles had conducted a service. She walked down to the aft well deck and strolled down the first-class corridor again towards the grand staircase. She ascended to the starboard A Deck, heading out to the promenade. She looked out the open window area and recalled Jack teaching Rose how to "spit like a man." She then looked back at the long promenade deck and remembered passengers flying down it into the water.

Pearl headed to the staircase that led to the forward starboard B Deck. She had a good view of the bow, forward well deck, crow's nest and bridge. Pearl took out the watch…11:30…ten minutes. Pearl had turned her camera off on the stern, but now had it out and pointed at her.

"April 14, 1912…11:30 p.m. Thirty-one degrees…all is quiet. The water…really does look like a mirror. It's almost peaceful, in a way. All I can do is wait for the first sight of the iceberg."

Pearl turned the camera off and peered into the distance. The night was calm and clear, yet somehow foreboding. It almost seemed too peaceful, as though Mother Nature herself were holding her breath in expectation.

Pearl's heart began to pound as she took one last look at the ship in its undamaged state. She glanced up at the bridge to see First Officer William Murdoch leaning on the railing. She looked at the crow's nest to see the two lookouts, Frederick Fleet and Reginald Lee, trying to keep warm.

Five minutes till…

Pearl stared at the horizon for the dark shape that would appear at any minute. She had her camera ready, and her heart was pounding hard by now. Suddenly, something took form in front of them, and Pearl's heart leapt into her throat. She turned the camera on.

"It's 11:35 p.m.," she told the camera. "I am officially the first to spot the berg."

She spun the glasses around to film the giant mountain of ice approaching and slipped them onto her face.

The iceberg appeared to be shaped like a crown. A peak rose in the center, curving down on either side to form two smaller, lateral peaks. The bow was pointed just to the left of the center peak, causing the majority of the iceberg's mass to fall on the starboard side.

No wonder Murdoch ordered a turn towards port, Pearl thought. *There's less iceberg towards port…topside, anyway.*

Pearl looked up at the bridge. Her memory flashed to her dream, where she alerted Murdoch to the impending disaster, and the *Titanic* turned in time.

If I shout out right now, all those people can be saved, she thought.

Pearl struggled with herself for a minute or so, watching as the iceberg drew steadily closer.

It's now or never, sister, Pearl thought, looking up towards the bridge.

Pearl opened her mouth to yell, but nothing came out. She looked back at the iceberg as her heart thudded inside her chest. Looking back up at the bridge, Pearl tried to force herself to call out. Pearl's heart wanted to save the passengers and the ship, but her mind would not let her.

Pearl looked back at the iceberg, closing her eyes resolutely.

No. I am here to observe, not to influence. I must not change history.

Pearl opened her eyes and looked up at the approaching iceberg five hundred yards away as her watch changed to 11:40.

Here we go... she thought.

Pearl heard three clangs of the bell in the crow's nest and looked up at the lookouts. A second later, she heard Fleet cry out, warning against impending tragedy.

"Iceberg, right ahead!"

Pearl looked up at the bridge to see Murdoch springing into action. He rushed to the wheelhouse, and Pearl heard him yell:

"Hard-a-starboard!"

After he had given the tiller order for an abrupt turn to port, he then rushed onto the bridge, dialing the telegraph to the engine room for full astern.

Pearl spun her head around to see the iceberg bearing down on them. She felt the engines slow as she white-knuckled the railing, bracing for impact. She could feel the engines reverse as they attempted to port around the berg.

Of course, turning an early twentieth century, steam-powered liner was not as easy as simply turning a steering wheel. People did not realize how much work moving the ship actually involved.

After the lookouts telephoned the warning to the bridge, the officer on duty signaled the engine room via the telegraph for full astern. Once the engine room received that message, the engineers sent another to the boiler rooms. The engineers shut down the engines to turn off the three propellers as the firemen closed the furnace doors on the boilers to dampen the fires and the quartermaster spun the wheel on the bridge to turn the rudder.

After the engines came to a slow stop, the starboard reciprocating engine would be engaged to turn the starboard propeller. The propeller would slowly rotate into action, causing the starboard side of the liner to move faster than the port side. Thus, the ship would turn to the left.

This procedure consumed the valuable time needed to avoid the iceberg, delaying the turn until it was too late.

"Helm's hard over, sir!" Sixth Officer James Moody alerted Murdoch, telling him the rudder could not turn any further. It was now all up to the propellers.

As the iceberg drew closer, the bow drifted inch by agonizing inch towards the left. The iceberg was less than one hundred yards away now.

"Oh, good heavens…" Pearl whispered.

A tear slid down Pearl's cheek as she waited for the defining moment. The tip of the bow cleared the ice to the left, and the ship looked like it was going to make it.

"Come on..." Pearl urged, willing the catastrophe away from them.

Although she knew it was unavoidable, she could not help but hope that it would not happen.

"Turn...turn..." Pearl begged, echoing Murdoch's wishes two decks up.

But the ship plowed on through the night, unaware of its own bleak future. The iceberg approached them, and as the bow pulled up alongside it, the inevitable finally happened.

The ice loomed closer, bringing with it a disaster that should never be forced on anyone.

Two seconds later, the iceberg collided with the starboard side below the water, tearing imperceptible holes in the iron hull. The berg bumped along, causing a horrific screech—not far from the sound of fingernails on a chalkboard—that faded into the still night. The metal against metal sound was only audible to those either up front or below deck. A shudder ran the length of the ship as Pearl felt the railing vibrate under her hands. The edge of the ship clipped the berg, causing ice to fall onto the forward well deck.

"Hard-a-port!"

As Murdoch ordered his command, Pearl rushed to the starboard railing to film the retreating berg. The iceberg was just outside the railing, and Pearl leaned over, brushing her fingertips against the cold ice. Despite the past five days, this one action made the tragedy of the *Titanic* so much more real than any picture could ever do.

As Murdoch closed the watertight doors, Pearl watched the iceberg pass by the stern. It looked almost serene and harmless, but the damage was already done. In three hours, the great "unsinkable" *Titanic* would be nothing more than a wreck on the bottom of the Atlantic.

"Full stop!"

Pearl looked up at the Boat Deck to see Captain Smith staring at the ice on the well deck, having just given Murdoch his order. The esteemed and experienced captain looked shocked and shaken, as though he had never seen anything like this in his life; which, in all truthfulness, he had **not** seen an event like this in his life.

As Smith left the railing to dress into his full uniform, Pearl turned back to the railing beside her. She leaned over and peered down at the bow, where she could imagine gallons and gallons of icy water were now pouring into the cargo holds and boiler rooms of the front five compartments. The water created a dark veil over the damage, hiding the catastrophe from any onlookers.

The irony of the situation was that if no preventative measures had been taken, the *Titanic* would have hit the iceberg head-on. Water would have filled only the front one or two compartments, allowing the *Titanic* to reach safety or stay afloat in time for a ship to arrive. Having turned to avoid a collision, the iceberg had trailed along the side of the ship, tearing a hole into five compartments. By trying to save the ship, they had only doomed themselves.

Some people might feel anger or hostility that something would dare destroy the *Titanic* like this. The truth is that the iceberg was completely innocent in this disaster. The *Titanic* had invaded its territory, the crew believing nothing could bring her down. Mankind had pushed their boundaries, and nature had merely pushed back, causing this tragedy that neither involved party anticipated nor expected.

Pearl turned away from the devastated bow and looked back down the long promenade. The greatest ship in history had just been irrevocably damaged by one of nature's most dangerous creations. The *Titanic* and the iceberg had spent years being formed in their separate worlds, and on this one night, the two leviathans had finally clashed and changed history.

16

Fatal Prognosis

Harold Bride made his way through the doorway into the Marconi Room. He saw Jack Phillips at his station, frantically trying to get out the rest of the passenger messages.

The poor guy looked exhausted. He had been at work all day, sending out messages and fixing the radio secretary that had burned out earlier that day. Even though his shift did not start for another ten minutes, Bride decided to be merciful.

"Why don't you go ahead and get some rest, Jack," said Bride. "I'll take it from here."

"Are you sure?" Phillips asked him.

"Yeah, I can start early," Bride told him.

"Alright," said Phillips, taking his headset off and holding it out to Bride.

Captain Smith stepped into the doorway, looking at Phillips. "We've struck an iceberg, and I'm having an inspection made to tell what it has done for us. You better get ready to send out a call for assistance. But don't send it until I tell you."

The captain left, and Phillips looked up at Bride, a frown forming on his face.

"An iceberg?" mused Phillips, a small smile finding its way onto his face. "I didn't even feel anything. I would have loved to have seen that."

Bride smiled and nodded as Phillips put his headphones back on. Bride sat down in the chair next to the operator's table, gazing at the doorway where the captain had stood a minute ago.

Was it really true? Had the ship really struck an iceberg? In all likelihood, they had. It **was** the North Atlantic in April at near midnight, and they **had** been getting several dozen reports the last couple of days about the ice. Maybe they should not have dismissed them right away. But then again…if it really was serious, wouldn't they be sinking right now?

"I wonder where it hit," said Bride.

"Well, it must have only grazed us," said Phillips, tapping out another passenger message. "Nothing seems to be amiss."

Just as that sentence escaped his mouth, they felt the engines cease their movement underneath them.

"Nothing amiss?" Bride asked Phillips with a brow raised.

"It's not our business to worry about," Phillips told him. "If something is wrong, the captain will tell us."

Reassured by his own infallible statement, Phillips went back to work.

~~

Captain Edward John Smith led the group of men into the chartroom, closing the door. Thomas Andrews immediately spread a blueprint of the ship onto the table. He and Captain Smith had just toured the forward lower compartments, taking in a damage report.

"How much total damage do we have?" asked Andrews.

"Water in the forepeak, the three holds and boiler room six," Smith told him.

Andrews' eyes went wide, and he looked down at the blueprint in shock.

"That's five compartments..." he breathed in stunned disbelief.

"Sir, if we open the pumps—" began Chief Officer Henry Wilde, trying to aid the situation.

"The pumps will only buy you a few minutes," Andrews announced. "They can't keep up with that much water." He took a deep breath and looked Captain Smith in the eye. "If any two compartments are breached, she can stay afloat long enough to reach safety. But not five."

Andrews looked back down at the blueprints, illustrating as he spoke. "The ship will go down by the head, water spilling over the bulkheads at E Deck."

"How long do we have?" asked Smith.

Andrews glanced up at Smith, eyebrows drawn together in worry. "Two and a half hours at the most. No matter what we do, *Titanic* will founder."

Smith let his mouth drop somewhat as he gazed at a cup of tea on the table across from him. The surface of the liquid tilted slightly in the cup, proving that the bow was already sinking.

"Mr. Murdoch," said Smith quietly.

"Yes, sir," came an equally quiet voice behind him.

Smith turned his head and looked at his first officer. "How many aboard?"

William Murdoch swallowed nervously, looking his captain in the eye. "Two thousand two hundred souls onboard, sir."

Smith looked back down at the blueprints, knowing rescue was impossible. No ship could arrive in two hours to save those that could not fit in a lifeboat. *Titanic* was on her own.

Smith turned back to look at Henry Wilde. "Ready the boats."

"Yes, sir," Wilde said, gesturing to Second Officer Charles Lightoller.

The two of them left the chartroom to begin uncovering the boats.

Smith took off his cap and stared at it. He knew that his crew would try, but it was useless. Half of the people in his charge would die tonight.

~~

Bride glanced around the wireless room, feeling a desperate need to do something. If they had struck an iceberg, hurried action was needed. Bride knew he was only a Marconi operator, and a co-operator, at that. There really was not much that he could do, which left him with a sense of hopelessness.

Captain Smith reappeared in the doorway, entering the Marconi Room. He looked wearier than when he had last been in the room, as though the weight of the world had come crashing down on him.

"Send the call for assistance," ordered Captain Smith. He grabbed the log book, writing on a small piece of paper and handing it to Phillips. "This is our position."

Bride glanced at the paper as Phillips took it from the captain. Smith had written the ship's coordinates down: 41°46′ North, 50°14′ West.

"We are going down by the head," Captain Smith continued.

"What call should I send?" asked Phillips.

"The regulation international call for help," replied Captain Smith. "Just that."

Phillips nodded, turning towards his station and beginning to send out "C.Q.D."

"Send 'S.O.S.,'" Bride spoke up. "It's the new call, and it may be your last chance to use it."

Phillips and the captain both laughed at that, despite the seriousness of the situation. Phillips turned back to his radio, tapping out the three dots, three dashes and three more dots repeatedly.

~~

Pearl jumped at the sound of a door opening.

Chief Officer Wilde and Second Officer Lightoller walked out with a small army of sailors. Lightoller headed portside as Wilde remained starboard. Wilde set his crew to begin uncovering the lifeboats. The sailors removed the canvas coverings as they had been ordered, unhooking the chains that held the boats in place. They quickly began attaching ropes from the davits to the falls that connected to the lifeboats.

Every sailor and officer now manning the lifeboats knew that the boats could only save half the ship. The new Welin davits had been installed to be able to load extra boats. The Welin davits could move back and forth, swinging from over the side of the ship towards the deck to lower more boats. The White Star Line had declined the extra boats, believing twenty was a sufficient number. After all, the law only required them to have sixteen aboard.

Another reason for the shortage of lifeboats was the manpower needed. If they gave the liner more lifeboats, they would be required to hire the number of sailors necessary to man and lower the extra boats. The White Star Line believed they had already made every possible precaution, and spending more money was unnecessary. Unfortunately for the 1,500 that could not fit in a lifeboat, money and luxury became the ultimate deciding factor.

The few passengers that had gathered on the Boat Deck began to return to the warmth and comfort of the lounge or grand staircase. The night air bit at the skin, making for an unpleasant time for everyone. And the engines were not helping.

Having come to a full stop, the engines were now blowing off steam through the relief pipes against the funnels as they cooled. The ship had been designed to blow off this steam when it was stopped to avoid overheating the engines. Every passenger on the ship would be thanking God for that small design idea. Water flooding an overheated engine room would surely have resulted in some type of explosion.

However, the noise that accompanied the front three funnels' steam roared through the night, drowning out all other noise. The crew had to yell in their comrades' ears to be heard. This intensified the noise level, causing passengers to withdraw to the quiet of the indoors where the band had begun to play lively ragtime music.

Leaving the ordered chaos of the lifeboats, Pearl retreated to the haven of the first-class lounge. She headed into the staircase, descending to A Deck and entering the lounge ahead of her. She entered a world entirely different from the one she had just left. Whereas the Boat Deck held a sense of barely perceptible danger, the lounge held an air of elegant celebration.

The band played music in the middle of the room, passengers mingled amongst themselves without a care, and stewards scurried among the crowd as they served drinks. The atmosphere of the moment felt like someone had decided to throw a party in the middle of the night.

Pearl vaguely noticed a lack of background noise coming from outside the windows. She headed back the way she had come, heading up the stairs to the Boat Deck. She walked across the room and through the door to the portside Boat Deck. As she walked through the door, she decided to turn the camera in her glasses on and keep it on the rest of the night.

The night was much quieter, the steam having died away from the funnels. Second Officer Lightoller appeared to be gathering the few passengers that had remained on the deck.

"For now, I need only the women and children to board the lifeboats, please," Lightoller called over the small crowd. "Please bring the women and children forward."

And with those words, the loading of the *Titanic*'s lifeboats began.

~~

People hustled out of the way, making room for Wallace Hartley and his band. They congregated portside in a small circle, looking to their leader for direction.

"*Maple Leaf Rag*," said Hartley, placing his bow to the strings of his violin.

The band struck up their strings, beginning the joyful piece to calm the passengers. The combination of the ragtime music and the slow loading of the lifeboats added a strange mix of panic and peace to the scene. It was sure to confuse more than a few people.

Here were these officers and sailors trying to load them into these tiny, little boats to save their lives. Yet, the orchestra played on as though there was no danger to be feared. Many did not want to leave the safety of this big, unsinkable liner and chance their lives out on the ocean in the small, rickety lifeboats. After all, the ship appeared to be perfectly fine.

Pearl watched many women scooting back towards the enclosed staircase and lounge, most seeking out their husbands. They obviously did not see the point of leaving.

This left Pearl with the sudden urge to rush headlong into the crowd with a cry of: "We're sinking! Get in the boats!" However, that would only serve to create mass hysteria. Besides, Pearl knew she could not interfere. Sometimes...you just have to let people go.

Pearl snuck past the crowds and approached the bridge, spotting Captain Smith emerging from the wheelhouse.

"Captain!"

Smith turned as Harold Bride rushed out of the corridor next to the wheelhouse.

"What is it, Bride?" asked Smith.

Bride handed Smith a piece of paper. "We have just received word from the *Carpathia*. They're the closest ship, and they're headed in our direction, full speed."

"Do they have an estimate for time of arrival?" asked Smith, still staring at the paper.

"They believe they can be here in four hours," Bride told him.

Smith's gaze flew to Bride, eyes wide.

Pearl knew what was going through his head right now. Andrews had given them a time limit of two and a half hours. The *Carpathia* would not reach the *Titanic* before it sank. Their last hope had just failed them.

Smith nodded. "Thank you, Mr. Bride."

Bride nodded and rushed back to his duty. Smith turned towards the nearest officer—Sixth Officer James Moody.

"Mr. Moody," commanded Smith. "Order the signaling rockets to the bridge."

"Aye, sir," said Moody. He immediately hurried to the bridge to call down for the rockets.

Pearl quickly made her way to an empty cabin on B Deck, changing out of her first-class dress and into a third-class one. Now wearing a plain green cotton dress and shawl for warmth, Pearl headed back to the crowded Boat Deck, observing the lifeboat loading process. It had taken her about fifteen minutes to change, and the lifeboats had begun to be filled.

It appeared that they were in the middle of loading Lifeboat Number Four. This boat held the most confusion of the night. During the course of the next hour, the boat would be lowered to A Deck to load at the promenade. However, the windows were closed, so it would be returned to the Boat Deck. Second Officer Charles Lightoller would then lower back to A Deck, thinking it would be easier to open the windows of the promenade deck. It would not be lowered until 1:55 a.m., leaving twenty seats empty in the rush.

Pearl headed through the foyer of the grand staircase, emerging onto the starboard Boat Deck. Directly in front of her, First Officer William Murdoch stood at the deck's edge at the center of Lifeboat Number Seven, arms stretched to each side to signal the seamen at the davits.

"Lower away!" Murdoch ordered.

Although the boat only contained twenty-eight people, it lurched violently as the sailors let the ropes slide through the davits.

Murdoch watched the progression of the boat down the side of the ship. "Steady..."

The davits shook as the ropes strained to lower the boat safely towards the water.

"Steady, men..." Murdoch ordered.

Once the boat reached the surface of the Atlantic, the crewman in charge—Lookout George A. Hogg—unhooked the falls with the help of two other crewmen in the boat. As Boat Seven drifted away from the liner into the dark sea, the sound of a cannon exploding drew the attention of everyone onboard.

Pearl glanced up to see the first rocket of the night exploding above the bridge. A shower of white sparks rained down towards the decks, creating a bright light that cast the scene in an eerie reality.

Something that was supposed to be beautiful was, in itself, a terrible omen. If anyone doubted the danger before, here was pure proof that something was amiss. The liner had only been equipped with eight rockets; they would not be wasted on something as trivial as a lifeboat drill.

Pearl glanced at the passengers around her, identifying the looks on their faces as they realized that the calm demeanor of the crew was all an act.

The ship really **was** sinking.

Their modicum of safety had just vanished into the night as surely as the iceberg had.

17

Lifeboats Away

Pearl walked over to the portside Boat Deck, heading forward one boat towards Lifeboat Number Six, which was just finishing being loaded. She spotted one of the women she had met, Helen Candee, climbing into the boat. Pearl stepped away slightly from the boat, not wanting Helen to recognize her now in third-class dress. Among the others in the boat were Margaret Brown, Lookout Frederick Fleet, and Quartermaster Robert Hitchens.

Pearl spotted J. Bruce Ismay standing near the enclosure of the grand staircase, watching the proceedings. Second Officer Charles Lightoller and Fifth Officer Harold Lowe bustled about, trying to prepare the boat for lowering.

Ismay looked forward at the bow, knowing it was lower than before, even though it was not perceivable yet.

"It's not enough…" said Ismay quietly. "It's not enough…" He rushed over to the lifeboat, pushing at the ropes and davits. "There's no time to lose! Lower away!"

Harold Lowe rushed over to him, pulling him away from the davits. "Keep back!"

"We must hurry!" Ismay emphasized. "Now, lower away! Quickly!"

"You want me to lower away quickly?" Lowe reprimanded. "You'll have me drown the whole lot of them! Now, back away and let us do our job!"

Ismay looked up at him in shock before looking at the seamen hurrying to ready the davits. He could see that he was in the way, which was only slowing things down. He nodded and backed away, resuming his former position at the grand staircase.

Charles Lightoller turned to his crew, who were just swinging the lifeboat over the side of the ship. He raised his arms to the men at the davits.

"Lower away!" Lightoller commanded.

Boat Number Six jolted as it began lowering.

"Lower away!" First Officer Murdoch called from the other side of the ship as Lifeboat Number Five was lowered.

Pearl moved through the atrium of the grand staircase and to the starboard Boat Deck, watching as Murdoch now began lowering Lifeboat Number Three. Sailors were busy loading Lifeboat Number One, which the Duff Gordons were now climbing into. Pearl knew Lifeboat Number Eight was being loaded on the portside. Boat Eight and Boat One would be lowered ten minutes from now.

Pearl glanced at her watch to see that it was one o'clock. Her mind began to spin.

How could an hour have passed already? Pearl thought. *The ship only has an hour and twenty minutes left!*

Pearl could only imagine the state of chaos below decks as the water climbed further and further. What it must look like to the passengers on the lower decks…

The water seemed to have a mind of its own, chasing passengers down corridors and up flights of stairs. Just knowing that the water was rising higher and higher, and they had nowhere to go. The terror of finding themselves standing at a locked gate as the water rose towards their heads…

Pearl quickly hurried back to the staircase, heading down to A Deck and rushing towards the staircase that led to the forward B Deck. Reaching B Deck, she descended to the forward well deck via a small staircase at the front railing. Hurrying through the gate and down the stairs, she raced across the wooden deck until she reached the opposite staircase. Climbing the stairs, she burst through the gate and emerged onto the Forecastle Deck. Approaching the railing of the prow, she leaned against the metal and peered over the edge.

Oh, how far away that water looked only twelve hours ago, Pearl thought.

When she had last stood in this location, the sun had bounced off the waves fifty feet below the deck. At the moment, water sparkled in the starry night ten feet below her. She glanced back at the name painted on the black metal to see the water licking at the yellow paint.

Watching very closely, she could see the water inching up the side of the ship, growing closer and closer to the deck.

~~

Thomas Andrews made his way through the crowd until he reached Charles Lightoller.

"What is the meaning of this, Mr. Lightoller?" Andrews demanded.

"We're busy, Mr. Andrews," Lightoller stated as he prepared to turn back to the half-filled lifeboat.

"I've just been to talk to Wilde about the half-filled lifeboats," Andrews continued, ignoring Lightoller's attempt to brush him off. "They were built for sixty-five people, but I've only seen about twenty in each boat!"

"You must understand," Lightoller told him. "These people don't want to board the boats. We've tried to get them in, but they are afraid."

"Then convince them!" commanded Andrews. "Force them, if you have to!"

"The boats may not be able to take the strain," skirted Lightoller.

"They were tested in Belfast with the weight of seventy men!" said Andrews. "For God's sake, fill the damn boats, Mr. Lightoller!"

Lightoller glanced back at the half-filled boat behind him before looking back at the terrified faces in front of him. He turned back to the crowd, raising his voice.

"Please! Women and children!"

He ushered more women into the lifeboat, filling it to its capacity. Once Lifeboat Number Ten was filled with fifty-five total passengers and crew members, Lightoller raised his arms to signal the seamen at the davits.

"Lower away!" he cried.

With Lightoller now loading the lifeboats to their capacity, Thomas Andrews headed down to the lower decks.

He rushed into the engine room, glancing around at the crewmen manning the pumps and electrical power. The engineers were trying to keep the water at bay for as long as they could and provide light for the crew and passengers to work by.

Andrews spotted several members of the nine-man Harland & Wolff Guarantee Group, of which he was also a member. The nine of them had been specially chosen to embark on *Titanic* from Belfast, Ireland, seeing to any problems or unfinished work. Three members of the group were helping the engineers with the pumps. Andrews spotted Anthony Wood Frost, the Foreman Fitter, among them.

"Archie!" Andrews called to him.

Frost looked at him and joined him on the platform, gripping the railing to stay upright on the tilting deck.

"How are the pumps fairing?" Andrews inquired.

Frost looked back at the working crew, taking a contemplative breath and looking back at Andrews. "They are workin' hard, but the watur is still risin'."

Andrews nodded, glancing at all the men still down here below decks and back at Frost. "The ship does not have much time to live, and if you stay here, you will die."

Several crewmen nearby overheard and glanced up with petrified gazes.

Frost sighed once more, looking at the water beginning to rise higher in the engine room. He nodded, seeming to talk himself into something. He looked Andrews in the eyes with a determined expression.

"We'll stay here as long as we need t' be here," Frost declared.

Andrews glanced around to see other engineers nodding their consent. Andrews felt a knot form in his throat as he stared at these men, so willing to stay behind to do all they could to give the passengers as much time as possible.

"Good luck, then," said Andrews, placing a hand on Frost's shoulder. "God be with you."

"An' wit' you," Frost assented.

Frost returned to his work at the pumps as Andrews headed back towards the upper decks.

~~

Pearl watched as the water crept up onto the deck of the prow. The most recognizable part of the *Titanic* wreck had just entered the water for the first time, where it would remain on the dark seabed, not to be seen again until discovered seventy-three years later.

Of course, the bow was the most recognizable part of the wreck. With the iceberg piercing the bow, water had time to seep slowly into the front of the ship, pushing all the air out towards the stern. The water pressure was equalized both inside and outside the ship as it sank, leaving the hull intact. The stern, however, was a different story.

Water did not enter the stern until after the breakup. The stern had sunk straight down, trapping air inside the hull. As the stern had sunk deeper, the air could not handle the pressure any longer and ripped the decks off the top of the ship, leaving the stern section mangled and strewn all over the ocean floor.

As each metal bar of the railing was submerged, the water slid along the decks towards the rest of the ship. Pearl backed away from the water, heading for the staircase back to the forward well deck.

After climbing down the stairs, she rushed across the forward well deck, checking her watch as she went. It was 1:25. Lifeboats Ten and Nine had been lowered five minutes ago, and Boats Thirteen, Eleven and Twelve had just been lowered.

Quickly, she made her way back towards the grand staircase.

18

Only Minutes Left

Pearl walked among the passengers near the fourth funnel as they were loaded into the boats.

"Get into the boat, Ida," came a male voice behind her.

Pearl turned to see an elderly couple standing near a lifeboat at the edge of the deck.

"No, Isidor," said the woman. "We have been living together for many years, and where you go, I go...As we have lived, so shall we die—together." She looked at the officer waiting for her to board. "I will not be separated from my husband."

Isidor slowly set his face and nodded.

"Please, sir," said a young woman in the boat, getting to her feet. "Please take my seat."

Isidor gently shook his head, motioning for the lady to take her seat once more. "No, I do not wish any distinction in my favor which is not granted to others."

Resolutely, the two Strauses made their way away from the crowd and towards their cabin.

Many couples, like Isidor and Ida Straus, did not want to be separated. However, the husbands gave the women no choice, refusing to watch their wives die with them.

As the boats were deployed, cries filled the night as women and children were lowered away from the men. Wives cried and mourned as they watched their husbands remain behind on the Boat Deck. Children cried as they screamed for their fathers. They could tell something was wrong and their fathers were not with them. The men, watching their families depart the ship, stood stoically on the deck, knowing they would never see each other again.

There was such a great divide between these two groups: the living departing in the boats and the dead waiting on the deck.

"Do you remember that day?" asked a man.

Pearl turned to see a middle-aged couple she did not recognize standing by the crowd around the remaining lifeboats. The woman had glued herself to her husband, tears falling down her face. The husband's arms looped themselves around her torso, holding her close to him.

"It was the summer of 1893," the man reminisced with his wife. "We decided to take in the fair. There was a tent where a gypsy woman told fortunes. We went inside, and she told us that we would be together forever."

The woman burst into fresh tears.

"And she was right," continued the husband, trying to be strong for the both of them. "We will be together forever. I will always be with you. No matter what happens tonight, no matter where you go, I will never leave you."

If it was possible, the wife clasped harder onto her husband, placing a ferociously desperate kiss on his lips. They broke apart and stared into each other's eyes, memorizing their faces for all eternity.

"I will never leave you," the man repeated. "Now go."

The woman hesitated, shaking her head slightly.

"Go," the man urged her.

"This way, madam," Fifth Officer Harold Lowe told the wife as he ushered her towards the half-loaded lifeboat behind him.

The wife reluctantly climbed into the boat, her eyes quickly finding her husband in the crowd as soon as she had been seated.

As Pearl turned towards the back of the ship, she spotted a small form scurrying by close to the ground. Pearl edged around the few people in front of her and gazed down at the deck. A knee-high, brown-and-black Airedale terrier ran past the crowd, searching for a safe haven.

That's the Astor's terrier, Kitty. The dogs must have been freed from the kennel already.

As Kitty made his way past the crowd, two more dogs appeared on the scene: a black-and-white French bulldog and a brown-and-white King Charles spaniel.

Pearl shook her head sadly at the fact that they would release the dogs from their cages and not the third-class passengers from the lower corridors.

Pearl jolted her attention back to the crowd.

The sense of panic had finally crept its way into the hearts of those on the decks. The passengers were beginning to push their way past each other, trying desperately to get to a boat. Even as the boats were being lowered, many tried to jump onto them, forcing the officers to employ the use of pistols in warning.

An outsider might have wondered what could have possibly driven these people to this level of aggression, shoving and scrambling toward a lifeboat to save themselves with total disregard for those around them. But Pearl understood what was driving these people: fear. Fear played with your emotions and twisted your logic until all rationality vanished from your mind, leaving you at the brink of desperation. These people were not angry or hostile...they were scared.

Fear had been working its way through the crowd steadily, sneaking among the passengers and looking for a crack to worm its way into the minds of those onboard. Having finally found those cracks, fear was now sinking its horrifying claws deep into their hearts. The results were startling.

"Get back!" Second Officer Lightoller yelled over the cries from the crowd, drawing his pistol and pointing it into the frenzy to keep them back from the boats. "Stay away! Women and children only!"

The crowd of men cowered away from the gun, becoming wary of the officer. Many looked as though they still wanted to rush the lifeboat.

Lightoller turned back towards the lifeboat, Number Fourteen, and nodded his head at Fifth Officer Lowe.

"Mr. Lowe, man this boat," ordered Lightoller.

Lowe immediately climbed into the boat.

"Alright," Lowe yelled over the passengers and seamen in the boat. "Nobody panic!"

Lightoller turned to the seamen at the davits. "Lower away!"

Lowe pulled out his own pistol, raising it into the air as the boat began its descent towards the water. As they passed the lower decks, passengers tried to jump into the boat, but Lowe waved his gun at them.

"Stay back!" Lowe yelled. "Keep out! Stay back!"

Lowe turned his pistol towards the air away from the ship and fired three times, warning the passengers away from the lifeboat. Fortunately, the passengers seemed to get the point, and no one was getting themselves shot.

Pearl looked at the stern-most lifeboat on the port Boat Deck as it was finishing up loading. Five minutes later, Lightoller stood in front of the boat and signaled the seamen at the davits once more.

"Lower away!" Lightoller commanded.

As Boat Sixteen began its descent to the water, Pearl walked around the raised roof of the first-class smoking room on the aft section of the Boat Deck. She headed over to Lifeboat Number

Fifteen, which was in the process of being lowered also. Pearl rushed over to the railing, looking down at the water.

Lifeboat Thirteen sat on the surface of the water as Chief Stoker Frederick Barrett tried to unhook the falls from the boat. The pumps, which had been steadily spewing water since the engines had stopped, had sent the lifeboat drifting aft. This left Boat Thirteen sitting directly underneath Boat Fifteen as it made its descent towards them.

"Stop lowering!" people in Boat Thirteen cried out to the people on the Boat Deck.

As Boat Fifteen neared the surface of the water, screams issued from Boat Thirteen as the firemen in the boat began cutting through the ropes. Eventually, the ropes were cut, and Pearl watched Boat Thirteen edge out from under Boat Fifteen.

Now that almost all the boats were gone, most of the crowd began making its way towards the stern. There were a fair few that remained up at the bow, waiting for the Englehart collapsible boats.

Pearl made her way towards the forward port Boat Deck, making it to the railing to see the forward well deck flooded with water.

It's happening too fast, Pearl thought. *We're sinking too fast. It's not enough time!*

Pearl looked at her watch, shocked to see there was only twenty minutes until two o'clock. She looked around at the many passengers still left onboard, tears forming in her eyes.

They really had no hope... she thought. *No matter how hard they tried...they were doomed from the start.*

"Lower away!" Second Officer Lightoller shouted from behind her.

Pearl turned to see the forward-most lifeboat, Number Two, being lowered with only twenty-five onboard. As the boat slowly disappeared over the side of the ship, Pearl recognized one of the passengers: Malvina Cornell. She had made it into a lifeboat. Pearl was able to breathe a sigh of relief at that small comfort.

~~

Harold Bride rushed along the corridor, heading back to the Marconi Room. He entered the doorway to find Jack Phillips still at his position at the radio, dutifully sending out messages to any ship that would listen.

Bride listened to the dashes and dots, making out the message: "Engine room full up to boilers."

Phillips stopped suddenly, listening through his headphones. "Bugger! I think I've lost them!"

"Who?" asked Bride.

Phillips looked quickly back at him. "The *Carpathia*. We must have lost our wireless."

"Well, then, there's nothing more we can do," Bride told him, holding out an extra lifebelt.

"Wait!" said Phillips, listening to his headphones again. "I'm picking up the *Olympic*."

He began quickly tapping out more messages while the wireless still worked.

Bride looked out into the corridor, watching the seamen that would dart by every so often. He looked back at Phillips, knowing his friend would not give up very easily. Bride admired Phillips for that unerring loyalty, staying at his post in the hopes of saving even just one more life.

Bride quickly approached Phillips and put the lifebelt on his friend and co-worker while he tapped away. Bride left the room, heading out to the Boat Deck to see if he could be of any help.

It was clear that the radio was quickly failing them. The ship could not hold out on the signal and electrical power; they would most likely lose radio contact soon. They had, after all, lost signal with the ship coming to rescue them. It would not be long until the signal completely stopped working. And when that moment came...the end would not be far behind.

~~

Pearl gazed out over the railing at the bow...the entirely submerged bow. The Forecastle Deck had sunk below the surface, and the water slowly crept up towards the promenade decks. The deck shimmered underneath the surface in the lights of the ship, appearing as an eerie mirage in an aquatic world.

Pearl turned back towards the port railing, watching as they prepared to lower the final forward port lifeboat, Number Four. This boat contained Madeleine Astor, Ida and Jean Hippach, and Eleanor Widener. After an hour, it was finally ready to lower.

"And lower away!" Lightoller commanded as the seamen fed the ropes through the davits and falls.

192

After Boat Four disappeared over the side of the deck, Pearl ran over next to the now-empty davits and gazed down at the water. Boat Four was already settling into the water, which was now only ten feet below the promenade.

Pearl could hear the officers and sailors hurrying to hook the collapsible boats up to the falls behind her, but her eyes stared transfixed at the glassy façade below her. It was now only a matter of minutes before the whole terrible ordeal drew to a close.

19

Death Throes

Pearl left the chaotic scene of the collapsible boats and headed for the grand staircase. She approached the railing directly ahead of the clock, gazing down into the well. The gravity in the tilted ship held her against the curved railing.

"Mr. Guggenheim!" someone called out.

Pearl looked down to see a steward holding out a lifejacket.

"I have a lifejacket for you, Mr. Guggenheim!" the steward told Benjamin Guggenheim.

Guggenheim and his manservant Victor Giglio stood on the stairs on the floor below her. Guggenheim held his hand out.

"No, thank you," he told the steward. "We are dressed in our best and are prepared to go down like gentlemen. No woman shall be left aboard this ship because Benjamin Guggenheim was a coward."

The two of them turned away from the steward and almost ran into another man.

"John," said Guggenheim.

John Jacob Astor looked up at him, slightly flustered.

"Where is Madeleine?" asked Guggenheim. "Is she safe?"

Astor stared at him. "Madeleine made it into a boat. There was no room for me."

Guggenheim nodded solemnly. "Good luck, John."

"Good luck," said Astor, giving a pat to Guggenheim's shoulder.

Astor pulled a cigarette out of his inside pocket, heading up the stairs towards the upper decks. The two passed each other, off to search for a safe haven.

Pearl made her way to the stairs, descending down to A Deck. She headed down the corridor ahead of the staircase, entering the first-class lounge. She made her way to the portside of the room, heading down another corridor and walking through the atrium of the aft staircase. Pearl headed through the doors into the first-class smoking room, turning the corner halfway into the room. The sight in front of her froze her to her core.

Thomas Andrews stood in front of the fireplace, his hands on the marble mantle as he stared at the floor. He pulled his pocket watch out, checking the time. As he slipped the watch back into his coat pocket, he opened the glass front of the clock on the mantle in front of him. He adjusted the time to 2:10.

Always the perfectionist, Pearl thought as she watched the solemn architect.

Even as the ship sank underneath him, Andrews wanted to keep the ship as perfect as he could. Having already failed the 2,200 people onboard with the sinking of the ship, Pearl could imagine that Andrews was striving to redeem himself by making sure everything else was in order until the ship finally went down. After all, his idea for more lifeboats had been vetoed, causing the loss of life that was now positive to happen this night. If the situation was not so dire, Pearl could imagine a giant "I told you so!" running through his head.

Andrews turned his head and spotted Pearl. His face looked absolutely devastated. His mouth drew itself into a thin line, his eyes were big and blank, and his eyebrows practically touched each other above his nose.

Pearl approached Andrews, placing a hand on his arm. "It's not your fault. You built a good ship...the greatest, most beautiful ship in history. Sometimes, bad things just happen."

"I should have found a way," muttered Andrews.

"There was nothing you could've done," Pearl insisted. "The ship was too big. Its rudder was too small. The iceberg was too large. The water was too calm to spot the breaking water at the base of the iceberg. It was a bunch of small circumstances that led to this. There was absolutely nothing that anyone could have done to stop it."

At this point, Pearl was trying to convince herself as much as she was Andrews.

Andrews nodded, accepting Pearl's point. A glass of brandy slid off of the mantle and crashed at their feet.

"You better go," Andrews told her.

Pearl nodded and headed for the doors. She stopped and looked back at Andrews one last time.

"I'm sorry," Pearl told him. "She truly is a beautiful ship."

Andrews gravely turned back to the fireplace, placing his shaking hands on the mantle and leaning his weary body against it.

Pearl turned and left the way she came. She made her way back through the smoking room, past the aft staircase, down the first corridor, through the lounge, down the second corridor, and into the grand staircase.

She made her way to the Boat Deck, heading for the collapsible boats on the port side of the ship. As she inched her way past the crowd, she spotted Captain Smith standing by the davit, staring at the scene. She watched as he caught sight of the women and children still left on the ship. He looked down at the collapsible boat—one of the last boats on the ship. He slowly turned and headed for the bridge.

Pearl followed him, staying a few feet back from him.

Smith gazed into the bridge, watching as the water made its way up the telegraphs and wheel. Smith walked towards the wheelhouse, closing the door behind him.

Pearl watched through the window as Smith took his place at the wheel, gazing out at the water in the bridge.

So, it's true, Pearl thought. *The captain **did** barricade himself in the wheelhouse. He went down with the ship.*

The captain was sealing his fate alongside the *Titanic*'s, unable to watch his majestic ship be torn asunder. He had failed…and now he would meet his end.

Pearl turned, leaving Captain Smith to his thoughts. She made her way aft towards the stern, having completed everything she had been assigned to do. Now…it was time to go down with the ship.

Cre-e-e-e-ACK!

Pearl halted as the sound echoed around her. It sounded like a tree falling in a forest. She looked into the vestibule of the grand staircase.

The water had reached almost to the top of the stairs, burying them in salt water. As people swam for safety, something shot up out of the water and froze. It was wood of some kind, and it was splintered at the top. The side that Pearl could see was in a zig-zag shape.

Almost like stairs…

Pearl suddenly realized what she was staring at: the grand staircase.

Of course…Now it all makes sense…

The staircase was made of wood, which is much less dense than water; that's why it floats. As water surrounded it, the wooden stairs had finally pulled away from the banisters to float to the surface.

That's why the staircase is missing from the wreck.

The staircase had broken free from its supports and risen to the surface of the water, breaking through the glass dome when the ocean engulfed the entire vessel. The staircase was probably scattered all over the ocean floor, or broke into smaller pieces and floated to shore somewhere.

Pearl frowned in sorrow, staring at the grand staircase. What a sad sight indeed, watching the ocean flood into this beautiful room that was never, ever meant to be touched by water.

The water had reached the Honor and Glory clock in the center of the staircase, which read 2:15. The water swallowed up the clock in its gaping jaws, freezing that moment in time for all eternity.

Pearl passed the grand staircase, dodging passengers all around her. Before she reached the next lifeboat davit, she jerked to a halt as she sensed that something was different. Something was definitely not the way it should be. After a moment, she realized what it was: silence. She had not really been listening to the music with all the chaos around her, but now she noticed the absence of the soft hum of notes.

Pearl slowly turned and gazed at the band.

Three members began to head aft as the band leader, Wallace Hartley, bade them goodbye. Hartley then turned to face the water as it climbed the deck and brought his bow to the strings. The soft, sorrowful notes of "Nearer, My God, to Thee" drifted over the passengers' cries and into the night.

The other violinists stopped and looked back at their friend. One by one, they turned to join their fellow man in death, saying their final farewell—their swan song. Just as the legend goes that a swan sings one beautiful song before it dies, so the band was performing their final piece in the most heartbreakingly beautiful song ever heard this night.

As they joined in unison, Pearl closed her eyes and began to sing under her breath along with them to the haunting melody.

"Nearer, my God, to Thee," Pearl sang in a whisper as hot tears trickled down her cheeks. *"Nearer to Thee. Even though it be a cross that raiseth me; still all my song shall be, 'Nearer, my God, to Thee.*

199

Nearer to Thee.' There let my way appear steps unto heaven. All that Thou sendest me in mercy given. Angels to beckon me; nearer, my God, to Thee. Nearer to Thee."

After a minute or so, Pearl noticed the water beginning to lick her heels. Pearl glanced down at the band and saw the water at their ankles. The violins' notes faded into the night as they ended their song, and Hartley glanced at the oncoming ocean.

"Gentlemen," he told them soberly, "it has been a privilege playing with you tonight."

Pearl watched as the band tied their instruments to their bodies, remembering solemnly that Wallace Hartley had been found with his violin strapped to his body, along with his music box.

Pearl wanted to stay and watch, but the water around her ankles told her the unrelenting ocean would not wait for her. Pearl followed the crowd as they rushed towards the stern.

Before this point, the passengers on the decks could kid themselves into hoping that the whole ordeal was part of their imagination: some horrendous nightmare that they would soon wake from. But nature did not lie. With the sight of the water creeping up the decks, the truth could no longer be ignored.

Pearl passed many people clinging to their loved ones: some poor, some rich, and some members of the crew. All now fighting for their lives; all doomed to die on this night. Society had tried for so long to define themselves by titles and labels. They had strived so hard to build the invisible social boundaries between them, but were now all united in a common goal: survival.

Looking at them now, Pearl recognized them for what they really were: nothing more than human beings trying desperately to cling onto life. Despite what they wanted to believe, from this night on, the seven hundred passengers in the boats would share a connection that no social class could erase: they were survivors.

Pearl raced along the deck and was startled when she bumped into someone. She turned her head and stared into her great grandfather's eyes.

Lachlan stared at her as he escorted Constance, baby in her arms, through the throng of people. He broke their gaze as he pushed past.

Other passengers near the deck railings hefted themselves over the barrier and plunged themselves through the air towards the water below. Many were resorting to this frenzied action; who knew why they were doing it. Maybe it was in desperation or lost hope. Maybe they thought they could survive if they ditched the dying ship right now. No one would ever really know.

People had always imagined the tragedy of the *Titanic* being calm and ordered, the people keeping their peace as they went down gracefully. The reality of the situation was much more frightening than anyone could ever truly imagine. How could someone go through this horrible fate and not run away screaming in terror?

As Pearl gazed back upon the waters rushing towards her, she saw the grand staircase dome engulfed in the arctic waters, probably breaking under the pressure. Beyond that, she could make out a chaotic scene around an overturned collapsible lifeboat. People were swarming the raft as water rushed past them.

Pearl heard a report like a pistol through the air, and she gazed up to see the cables supporting the first funnel snapping under the pressure.

The hull stretched as it sank, opening the expansion joint behind the first funnel further every minute. The cables strained against the tension, finally breaking.

Collapsible Boat A floated in the water on the starboard side of the funnel. The people who had congregated around the lifeboat now floated in the water around it, including those who had helped to ready the boat.

The last of the cables snapped, and the funnel fell towards the water on the starboard side, collapsing onto the floating passengers. A wave of water surged up on either side of the funnel, rushing towards other passengers and boats. The funnel began to sink as Pearl watched, knowing who had been standing in the crowd the funnel had just fallen on.

So, that's what happened to Murdoch, thought Pearl. *He was crushed by the funnel.*

Pearl proceeded towards the aft well deck, brushing through the many people in front of her as she climbed down the stairway. Pearl continued to push through the crowd around her, trying to make her way to the stairwell to the stern.

As she rushed, the lights all over the deck began to fade, but swiftly returned to their full, bright glare. The breakers down below in the engine room were trying to compensate for the water and tilt of the ship. Pearl knew they could not possibly last much longer.

Pearl grabbed onto a railing, taking note of the tilting angle. If she had to guess, she would put it at forty degrees. She did not have much longer until the break of the hull. If she was not at the stern railing by that time, she would have no hope of guaranteed survival. Sure, she might make it from other parts of the stern, but that was only a guess. Not to mention there were a number of things that could happen if she were not on the stern. She could get hit by something, a part of the ship—like, say, a funnel—could fall on her; anything could happen. The safest place on the sinking ship was the stern railing. With this crowd around her, she had no hope of reaching the fantail in time.

As she began to lose hope, she glanced down at the locket around her neck. She grasped it, closing her eyes and remembering Sam as she saw him last: standing behind the observation window. She remembered her dream the other night: Sam slipping from her grasp as they struggled in the cold water.

"You can make it, Pearl."

Pearl opened her eyes to see Sam standing on the raised deck above the crowd. He was slightly transparent, as though he was not really there. He was speaking to her.

"I know you can make it...I'm waiting for you," Sam encouraged. He smiled down at Pearl and extended his hand. "Come home."

Pearl smiled and reached her hand out. "Sam..."

As Sam faded from her sight, Pearl kept extending her hand and grasped onto the railing in front of her. With a new fervor, Pearl surged forward into the crowd. She pushed her way through the people, squeezing into whatever spaces she could find. She found her way to the staircase and quickly followed the person in front of her up.

Pearl emerged onto a slightly less crowded deck, where passengers clung to anything bolted down. As she forced her way to the middle of the fantail, a loud voice came to her over the din of screaming voices. She turned towards the center of the deck and saw Father Thomas Byles conducting a service, surrounded by many third and second-class passengers, even a few first-class.

"And I saw a new heaven and a new earth," Father Byles recited to the small crowd in front of him as he clung to the capstan behind him for support, "for the first heaven and the first earth were passed away; and there was no more sea. And I John saw the holy city, New Jerusalem, coming down from God out of heaven, prepared as a bride adorned for her husband. And I heard a great voice out of heaven saying, Behold, the tabernacle of God is with men, and he will dwell with them, and they shall be his people, and God himself shall be with them, and be their God. And God shall wipe away all tears from their eyes; and there shall be no more death, neither sorrow, nor crying, neither shall there be any more pain: for the former things are passed away.[6]

"Whither shall I go from thy spirit? Or whither shall I flee from thy presence? If I ascend up into heaven, thou art there: if I make my bed in hell, behold, thou art there. If I take the wings of the morning, and

---

[6] Revelation 21: 1-4

dwell in the uttermost parts of the sea; even there shall thy hand lead me, and thy right hand shall hold me.[7]

"The Lord is my shepherd; I shall not want. He maketh me to lie down in green pastures: he leadeth me beside the still waters. He restoreth my soul: he leadeth me in the paths of righteousness for his name's sake. Yea, though I walk through the valley of the shadow of death, I will fear no evil: for thou art with me; thy rod and thy staff they comfort me. Thou prepares a table before me in the presence of mine enemies: thou anointest my head with oil; my cup runneth over. Surely goodness and mercy shall follow me all the days of my life: and I will dwell in the house of the Lord for ever."[8]

As Pearl watched the people tearing past her, she knew she had to keep moving; she could not stay watching a moment longer. She scrambled up towards the stern, remembering the dream she had been having back in 2005 over and over again.

She abruptly caught flashes skimming through her mind, brought on by her terror: the blind panic as she reached for the railing, her numb fingers struggling to keep a hold of the railing as she dangled from the stern, the startling realization that she was going to die as her purchase slipped and she fell towards the cold ocean…

She knew that she could not let that happen; she had to survive.

Pearl clung to anything that offered a handhold in order to pull herself against gravity. The deck had reached a forty-five degree angle, and bangs and thumps could be heard under their feet. Pearl's feet slid several inches, and she flung her hand out, catching the metal

---

[7] Psalms 139: 7-10
[8] Psalm 23

leg of a deck bench. She used it to steady herself and continued walking.

Pearl took several breaths and burst into a run, using her momentum to carry her up the deck. As her feet began to slip, she raised both arms and grasped the air with her hands. As she fell, her hands fell on a metal bar. She whipped her head up to find her hands wrapped around a bar of the stern railing. She smiled as she used her arms to pull herself towards the railing. She stood up, swinging her right arm over the outside of the top of the railing.

Pearl looked over the stern and down to the water below. Many white dots floated on the surface; the passengers in lifebelts looked so small and far away. Much debris floated among the passengers: chairs, crates and anything that could float. It had all been tossed overboard, most likely by a kind soul trying to provide something for the others to cling to in the water. Further away from the doomed ship floated a dozen or so lifeboats, slowly rowing away for fear of the ship sucking them under.

The rudder and propellers had risen out of the ocean, dripping with water. The new brass shone in the light from the stars. Perhaps that was why the ship looked so beautiful, even as it sank: the ship was brand new with not a blemish on her.

The lights on the ship faltered once again, bringing Pearl back to the moment.

Pearl could see the stern still rising steadily into the dark sky, hanging in the air in a monumental defy of gravity. She could imagine the passengers seeing the danger all around them and clinging to the one thing that should mean certain safety when it was the one thing

206

that meant certain death. It seemed a cruel sort of irony: clutching to the ship for safety as it dragged them under.

They knew they needed to ditch the ship, but there was absolutely nowhere to go. The utter hopelessness they all felt in this situation...to be in this moment right at the end on the edge of the railing, looking down at that big, black ocean with one decision in front of them...stay with the sinking ship...or jump into the freezing waters.

Which do they choose?

Even at that moment when surrounded by certain disaster, it still seemed unbelievable that this was happening...that such a wonder of a ship could become such a monster. If not for the complete reality of the moment, one could imagine it was all a terrible Greek tragedy thought up by some playwright. But the horror of the story was that it was not a story at all...it had actually happened...

...**was** happening.

And nothing could stop it.

"This isn't happening..." a man next to her pleaded as he shut his eyes tight and shook his head. "This isn't happening..."

But it was happening...and he knew it.

Even so, Pearl desperately prayed that she would snap awake to find herself in her comfy bed at home in her time. She had been dreaming about dying on the *Titanic* for a couple weeks now, but unlike her dreams, she knew that, this time, it was real. Even in a person's dreaming state, there is a voice in the back of their mind that suggests that the vision they are seeing is a dream. Now, however, there was only deathly certainty that no one on this ship would suddenly wake from this horrible nightmare.

Pearl clung to the railing and looked up at the man next to her. He was dressed in a white tunic uniform with a life vest over his outfit. It was Chief Baker Charles Joughin. He pulled a flask from his pocket and took a huge drink.

Pearl spun her head to look at the couple next to her.

Constance had one arm around Lachlan's midsection and one arm cradling their son. Lachlan, in turn, had one arm around Constance and one around the railing. Constance looked at the woman next to her, who was holding a small girl.

"Don't worry," the mother whispered to her daughter as she sobbed. "It's almost over. I promise it's almost over."

Constance looked over to her other side, and her eyes caught Pearl's and held them. A couple of tears ran down her cheeks as she recognized Pearl.

Constance's stare was interrupted as a terrible groan rang under their feet.

The stern tilted even steeper, causing everyone to grab on harder to whatever lifesaver they could reach. People slipped down the deck, sliding down to the bottom or ricocheting off of obstacles. They did not look like human beings in charge of every force in the universe. They looked like puppets flopping about on their strings, their every movement and action determined by something larger than they can comprehend.

A deep groan traveled the length of the *Titanic*, from one end to the other. The ship was trying so hard to remain intact, to go down with some dignity. Pearl heard several loud bangs and scrapes as everything that was not bolted down slid towards the bow. Several crashes were heard as either glass or china—most likely both—began breaking as it collided with other objects.

As Pearl began to think of Sam and how she longed to see him once more, the lights all over the ship flickered once…

…twice…

…and died, plunging the scene into darkness. Now the only light on the ocean was the stars that sparkled serenely in the night sky. They would be the only witness to this tragedy; them and the icebergs.

Pearl's heart stopped as the hull began to groan, the *Titanic* voicing her indignation about the atrocious mistreatment. She knew what would come next. After trying to hold a megaton stern one hundred and fifty feet in the air, the hull could not support her a second longer.

The *Titanic* was breaking in two.

Pearl wrapped her other arm around the railing as a great explosion ripped the silence of the night. The ship faltered a little as the hull started to splinter, the only thing holding her together being the keel. Her stomach shot up into her chest as the ship fell underneath her. Screams rose from those onboard as the ship pulled them back towards the ocean.

For a few brief moments, Pearl was engaged in free fall as the stern plunged back onto the ocean. A giant tidal wave flew out on either side of the hull as Pearl held onto the railing, bracing herself. As the stern met the water, Pearl slammed onto the deck, unaware that she had left it. Her arms slipped from the railing as the ship bobbed underneath her stunned body.

Momentary confusion and relief flooded the passengers. It was as though nature had changed its mind, correcting its mistake and saving the *Titanic*. It became rapidly evident that was not the case as the final funnels crashed to the deck, toppling over the side into the water.

The stern settled on the water, and they lay still for about thirty seconds before the bow, which was still connected to the stern at the keel, began to pull the stern with it as it went under. Water began to seep into the broken section, and slowly, the stern began to rise into the air once again. This time, the stern started tilting faster.

Pearl scrambled up to the railing once again as the stern quickly reached thirty degrees. Pearl swung her left leg over the railing and planted her foot on the deck again. Her right leg followed as she turned around, face down on the railing. The stern was at forty-five degrees and going fast.

Pearl heard a woman gasp, and she looked to her right to see Constance struggling to climb over with the baby in her arms. Lachlan could not do much to help, so Pearl hooked her foot through the railing and leaned over.

"Let me help!" Pearl called over the noise.

Lachlan looked up at her and nodded.

Pearl threw her hands out towards Constance. "Give me the baby!"

Constance raised her arm, and Pearl dug a hand under the bundle of blankets. She wrapped her other arm around the baby and pulled him towards her chest.

As Lachlan grabbed Constance's newly free arm, Pearl gazed down at her grandfather. He had been crying, but he now looked up at Pearl, serene and quiet. For a minute, the reality of the moment melted away as she looked at this innocent being in her arms.

"Sean…" Pearl whispered as she smiled at him.

Lachlan pulled Constance over the railing, and she turned to Pearl.

"Thank you," Constance told her.

Pearl leaned towards her and handed the baby to her.

"Good luck," said Pearl.

Pearl grabbed the railing once again as the ship came to a rest at ninety degrees. The bow had detached from the stern, sinking towards its watery grave bed. The two were now separated forever, never to be one again.

Pearl looked straight down at the churning water below her, terrified beyond anything.

"Help!"

"Someone, help!"

Many people hung from railings, benches, capstans and poles. They tried to hold on, but their grip slipped, and they fell into the ocean. Some hit the metal structures on the deck, their bones most likely fracturing upon impact.

The night had grown silent, save for the screams, and Pearl took those few moments to look around.

The sky was clear and sparkling like diamonds. The horizon was flat and empty, a lonely, calm ocean all around the ship. Small lifeboats floated every thirty feet or so in the water, keeping the *Titanic* company until her final throes.

Pearl looked up at the sky, the stars shining down. The scene around her suddenly seemed so microscopic compared to the infinite universe above her; an event so large and yet so small.

Pearl suddenly remembered Sam—her Sam, the one constant in this madness. The one who had promised, with a gift, that he would always be with her. She reached under her clothing and grasped the precious locket. She opened it up to look at the picture.

Sam appeared so happy and carefree; the curve of his smile, the sparkle in his young eyes, the dimple always present on his cheek. A tear fell down Pearl's face as she gazed at that moment that seemed like an eternity ago. It was a stark contrast to the moment Pearl found herself in now.

Pearl smiled as she closed the locket and pictured his face.

My Sam...

The sound of metal creaking pulled Pearl's attention back down to 1912.

The stern slowly began sinking into the water. Pearl sat on the railing, riding the ship down like an elevator. A terrible groan emanated from the hull as the metal shifted against the rivets. Pearl unhooked her foot from the railing and braced herself. She knew there would be no suction that would pull her under, so she got her feet under her and just waited.

Pearl began to get goose-bumps, and her stomach seemed to clench as she thought about how cold that water would be. Her wetsuit would not have held out for very long if they had not installed a heating unit inside. However, her feet, hands and head would still be exposed.

A torrent of water burst out of the aft cargo hatch as the pressure inside built to a climax. An explosion of air and water shot out of the hatch until it sunk under the surface. The churning water reached the main deck as Pearl's rate of breathing quickened.

As the water drew closer toward her, she could feel the spray of the sea on her face. Her skin tingled where the small droplets landed. The roar of the ocean overcame the groaning of metal on metal as Pearl stood up halfway on the railing. As the stern sank into the water, Pearl's body submerged itself into the icy waters.

Pearl gasped in shock at the cold. *Yep, a thousand knives all over my body...*

Pearl bobbed on the surface of the Atlantic, the frigid water triggering the heating element in her wetsuit. The water churned all around her as she tried to keep her head up. After a second, she took a deep breath and plunged her head into the icy waters. She clamped her glasses to her face to keep them on and peered into the darkness below her.

Slowly creeping its way into the fathomless depths, the stern shone in the icy blue of the ocean. This was the last time it would be seen by human eyes, and Pearl wanted to watch until darkness consumed the broken hulk of a liner.

The yellow letters emblazoned on the black iron jumped out of the eerie environment, adding a sense of irony to the whole situation. The name had been chosen for the liner's size, strength and luxury. Now, the name *Titanic* glared mockingly at Pearl, conveying tragedy, loss and disaster. As the liner sank deeper and deeper, the ghostly name gleamed through the watery depths before fading into black.

20

Floating Graveyard

Pearl pushed through the surface and sucked in a deep breath, the cold oxygen nearly freezing in her throat and lungs.

People thrashed in the water around her, creating mass chaos all around them. No one paid any mind to anyone else; their thoughts were only on their own peril and survival. It was amazing how the cold water could just shut everything else out. Arms flailed in every direction, screams flew from every mouth, legs kicked relentlessly against the water, and struggling bodies churned the water into one massive whirlpool.

"Help! Someone, help me!"

"Help us! Please, God, help us!"

Yells and cries came from the fifteen hundred people in the ocean with her. Some had lifejackets strapped around their torsos to keep them afloat. Others scrabbled for any floating item to grab onto, sometimes fighting amongst themselves for it.

Pearl watched the crowd of passengers that spread for about eight hundred feet in length. The floundering passengers with their lifejackets appeared to be an eerie, floating graveyard in the still night.

Pearl slowly swam for the edge of the floating masses, searching for a patch of clear ocean. An icy burn began to sear her scalp as her wet hair slowly began to freeze in the arctic air around her. Coming to the edge of the chaotic crowd, she proceeded to bring her legs to the surface, laying back and distributing her weight throughout her body. As she balanced her buoyancy, she floated on her back to save her physical strength.

Pearl heard a strange noise to her right, and she turned her head slightly to look at the source of the noise. A small King Charles spaniel swam through the icy waters, whining in pain as he moved through the water. Pearl watched him go until he was out of sight, and she turned her head back towards the sky.

Pearl found herself staring at the stars as they twinkled in the ink-black sky. A band of clouds and gas stretched across the stars: the Milky-Way. It was all so clear and stunning. She was once again struck by the extent of the situation. The stars hung in a vast universe millions, even billions, of miles away from the miniscule blue planet where this immense disaster had just occurred.

Pearl slowly brought a hand to her chest, careful not to disrupt her equilibrium. She pulled her necklace out from under her shirt, clasping it in her hand.

"You did it, Sam..." Pearl whispered through time and space, reaching out to the man that she loved. "You saved me."

The seconds turned into minutes, and the minutes turned into hours. Pearl floated on the ocean's surface, constantly moving her feet, toes, fingers and hands to keep the circulation going.

Little by little, the screams died down into weak cries, which slowly filtered away as the hypothermia claimed them. The cessation of the ghastly wails brought an odd sense of relief that Pearl was ashamed to admit.

Pearl looked at her watch: 2:47 a.m. Pearl let her lower body sink, and she made her way back to the crowd.

Bodies in white, cork-filled life vests floated on the surface, heads cocked to the side in dreamless, eternal slumber. Pearl clamped back the tears that threatened to spill from her eyes and freeze on her face.

Movement about twenty feet to her right caused Pearl to move to the nearest body to hide behind. She peered out as a baby's cry came through the air.

Constance weakly made her way through the water, holding her baby high above the surface. Her arm was slowly dropping, but she tried with all her ebbing strength to keep her son from the killing waters. She was still twenty feet from the suitcase that Sean was meant to be found in, and Pearl could see that Constance was slowly losing.

But how can that be? Pearl wondered, confused. *If Sean really did die that night, I wouldn't be here. Maybe someone helped her.*

Pearl looked around, but saw no movement anywhere.

There's no one to help! Unless...

216

Pearl suddenly remembered how Elizabeth Vandez had described the woman that came into the orphanage with Cecily.

"You have her eyes. And that beautiful face with her ruby red hair...she was an angel."

Pearl had a sudden revelation that Elizabeth had described *her*. She remembered how she had helped Constance over the railing on the stern. She had already meddled with history, but if she hadn't, Constance never would have gotten onto the stern, and Sean would have died. But he had survived...because of her...

Pearl darted forward just as Constance's arm fell towards the water. Pearl reached out with her hands and caught her grandfather before he touched the water.

Constance looked up at her through half-lidded eyes, recognizing her. "Thank...you..."

"You're w-welcome," shivered Pearl as she held Sean with one hand and used the other to clamp Constance's hand onto Pearl's dress.

Pearl used her legs and free arm to swim towards the suitcase. She looked inside to find that the shell of the suitcase had not allowed any water to leak inside.

Inside on the bottom of the suitcase laid the three items. The blue blouse had elbow-length velvet sleeves with a slight poof in the shoulders. The velvet collar ran up to the chin, but the rest of the blouse consisted of a satin-like material for the torso and shoulders. Buttons fastened the front of the blouse down the middle.

Next to the blouse lay the purse. It was a rust orange felt material with a carved brass clasp on the top, and a gold chain attached to the top to carry it.

The bracelet had fallen out of the purse and was lying on the floor of the suitcase. It was a gold, expandable band with carved detailing, and an orange-colored, heart-shaped jewel sat in the top of the band.

Pearl carefully laid the baby in the suitcase, making sure it still floated. Constance peered over the edge at her small boy, tears in her tired eyes.

"Your s-son is g-gonna live a long, f-full, happy life," Pearl told her. "He's g-gonna f-find a w-wonderful f-family to love him. One d-day, he'll m-meet a w-woman and g-get m-married, and they'll have k-kids of their own."

"How...do you know...tha'?" Constance muttered weakly.

Pearl took notice of her lack of shivering; the hypothermia had fully set in. Pearl saw no harm in revealing the truth. After all, Constance was about to die. And she would likely believe Pearl, what with the hypothermia disorienting her mind.

"B-Because I'm your g-great granddaughter," Pearl told her. "I t-time traveled here." Pearl opened her locket to show her the modern photograph. "S-See?"

Constance focused on the picture of the two of them and smiled. "Is tha' yur husban'?"

Pearl smiled. "M-Maybe someday...I hope."

"Whaz 'is name?"

"S-Sam W-Wyatt."

"Sam...Sam 'n Pearl. So beau'iful..."

Pearl smiled sadly at her. "You r-rest now. I'll w-watch over my g-grandfather till the ship c-comes."

Constance nodded and closed her eyes, slipping away. As Pearl watched her great grandmother floating on the surface of the water in her lifejacket, she reflected on what had just happened.

If I hadn't been here to save Sean, I wouldn't even be here in the first place.

Pearl had been destined to travel here to this time since before she had been born. If she had not time-traveled to the *Titanic*, Sean would have died on this night, and her family would have never existed. Pearl had been to 1912 and saved her grandfather before Kyle had even discovered time travel.

Man, that could give you a headache...

Pearl jolted her gaze away from her grandfather as she heard a voice calling over the water.

"Is anyone there?! Can anyone hear me?!"

Pearl moved to the side of the trunk to see around it, spotting a lifeboat making its way through the bodies.

Bodies...

Pearl cringed at that thought and looked around to see if anyone else was moving. She could not be rescued before someone else; it could mean the difference between life and death. The longer a person stayed in the freezing water, the more chance that someone meant to survive would die.

Pearl could see no one moving and knew it was time to get rescued. She knew that when a person suffering from hypothermia ceased movement and fell unconscious, there was no recovery possible for them; at least, no recovery possible in this decade.

Medical procedures for hypothermia would not be developed until much later.

"Here!" Pearl called, waving her hand in the air. "I'm here!"

"Come about!" shouted the officer in charge—Fifth Officer Harold Lowe. "Row over there, men!"

Pearl kicked her legs behind her in the water, careful not to breach the surface and splash the infant. She kept a hand on the suitcase as she slowly moved through the water. She reached the lifeboat as the sailors retracted the oars. The men put their arms down to help her up, but Pearl shook her head fervently.

"Him f-first," Pearl told them as she slid the suitcase towards them.

Unable to reach the child, they grasped the leather straps and heaved the whole suitcase into the boat. They reached down again, and Pearl grasped onto their jackets. One of them gripped her cloak and pulled, lifting her from the water. Pearl swung her leg over the edge of the boat, tumbling into it.

The sailors helped her up, setting her on one of the seats and wrapping a blanket around her. Pearl looked across from her and spotted a familiar face peeking out from a blanket. Cecily Miles caught her gaze and offered a weak smile.

"Miss, your baby."

Pearl looked up at the sailor standing next to her. He held the baby out to her, wrapped tight in a second blanket. Pearl wanted nothing more than to take her grandfather in her arms and protect him, but she knew her part was done.

"He's not m-mine," Pearl stated sadly.

The sailor stepped back and looked down at the sleeping boy in his arms, wondering what to do now.

"Give him here," Cecily stated, opening her blanketed arms.

The sailor stepped over and handed the baby to her, scooting back and settling back into his place at the oars. Cecily held Sean close to her, smiling as he opened his eyes and gazed up at her. Cecily looked up at Pearl.

"Thank you," Pearl told her.

Cecily frowned. "What for?"

"F-For loving him enough," Pearl told her, curling the blanket tighter around her.

"You're welcome...I think," said Cecily, turning her attention back to the child in her arms.

Pearl looked down at her feet as they drifted in the ocean, waiting for the *Carpathia* to arrive.

21

Memorial at Sea

Lifeboats drifted in various places on the ocean surface, surrounding a field of debris and lifebelt-clad bodies. Pearl could not see the white boats, but they were there.

Pearl looked at Cecily, who was gently bouncing Sean in her arms.

"Why didn't you get onto a lifeboat when they were being loaded?" Pearl asked.

Cecily looked up from the infant's face. "I did not feel comfortable saving my own life when there were still many onboard. If they were going down, I was going down with them."

Pearl smiled, grateful that Cecily had thought about others, even while her own life was at stake.

Harold Lowe suddenly grabbed a flare from the emergency box in the bottom of the boat. He lit the top of it, waving it back and forth.

Pearl sat up straighter, gazing into the distance. A liner was making its way towards them, its lights shining in the darkness.

Pearl smiled a little as she recognized the ship. *It's the* Carpathia...

The seven hundred in the boats had drifted for about an hour, waiting for rescue. It was isolating, being stranded in the middle of the Atlantic while the waves grew steadily stronger. The passengers sat in the cold boats, not knowing if their family and friends had survived. Maybe they made it to a boat. Maybe they had succumbed to the frigid waters in the icy graveyard. Maybe they had gotten trapped in the ship as it sank below the surface. They had no way of knowing until they boarded the *Carpathia.*

The *Carpathia* had come to a drifting stop amid the boats. One by one, the boats pulled alongside the ship. A rope ladder was lowered towards the boats for passengers to climb up. Several passengers could not climb, and the officers had to use a bosun's chair, which the passengers sat in to be hoisted up the side of the ship.

The sky had lightened to a blue-black by the time Pearl's boat was rescued a few hours later, casting the faintest of light onto the tragic scene. By the time the sun rose, Pearl was watching the officers of the *Carpathia* pull the rest of the passengers up to the deck.

Pearl watched as women and children, even some men, made their way across the decks. They appeared disillusioned, as though the veil hiding them from reality had been crudely ripped away. Their faith in the human dominance of the elements had been shaken to its core, leaving an astounded and traumatized world in its wake. Nothing they knew would ever be the same.

Finally at 8:30, the final boat to be rescued was being unloaded, and the officers of the *Carpathia* began making preparations to head to New York.

As the crew of the *Carpathia* hauled Harold Bride onto the deck, Pearl rushed forward to help. As a team, they got him into their arms and began heading towards an empty cabin. Bride was laid on the couch, and a blanket was thrown over him.

Bride looked up at Pearl. "Hey, I know you. You're the reporter with Mr. Andrews."

Pearl nodded, smiling. "I'm sorry about your feet."

Bride looked down at his broken, mangled feet. "Thank you." He drew the blanket up across his arms. "I'm glad to see you made it."

"You, too," said Pearl, covering his feet with the blanket to keep them warm. "Have you seen your operator friend?"

Bride looked down at the floor solemnly. "Jack made it to a lifeboat, but died during the night from cold exposure."

"I'm sorry to hear that," Pearl offered. She stood, giving him a sympathetic smile. "I hope you feel better."

"Thank you," said Bride.

Pearl left the room, heading back to the main deck.

"That was very hospitable of you," came a voice to Pearl's left.

Pearl turned to see a young woman in a stewardess uniform. "Thank you. He looked like he needed help."

"Well, I'm sure he appreciated it," she said.

Pearl smiled at the stewardess, extending her hand. "Pearl Liberti."

The stewardess accepted the proffered hand. "Violet Jessop."

Pearl recognized the name. Violet Jessop had been a stewardess on the *Olympic* when it collided with the H.M.S. *Hawke*. She had obviously survived the *Titanic*'s sinking, and she had moved on to become a stewardess on the *Britannic* when it struck an underwater mine and sank.

"You know, this is the second nautical disaster I have been onboard to witness," said Violet. "It's strange how life works out."

"It's about to get stranger," muttered Pearl.

"What was that?" asked Violet.

"It's good we're out of danger," Pearl told her, correcting her mistake.

"Yes," said Violet. "I can't imagine going through this a third time."

Pearl watched sadly as Violet turned towards the passengers, seeing what help she could provide. Unfortunately, Violet's full experience with tragedy was still waiting for her in the near future.

Violet was not the only one with this misfortune. Arthur J. Priest served as a fireman on the three Olympic-class ships: *Olympic*, *Titanic* and *Britannic*. Unlike Violet, Arthur worked on the ships *Alcantara* and *Donegal*. Both ships had been torpedoed and sunk by German submarines during World War I. After this fifth disaster, Arthur had to retire because no one would serve on the same ship with him.

Pearl walked to the railing on the deck, looking out into the eerie waters. Debris and bodies littered the surface of the ocean a few hundred feet away. The final lifeboat slowly made its way up the side of the *Carpathia* as it was pulled onto the deck.

Pearl took a moment to say a prayer for those who now lay in their watery graves…both those on the surface and those inside the ship now two and a half miles below her feet.

~~

After a memorial service held on the decks of the ship, Pearl stood at the stern railing as the *Carpathia* sailed away from the accident site. The passengers of the deceased *Titanic* were leaving behind the ship and the dead and the whole horrid night. Many wished they could leave their emotions and mourning behind as easily as coming about and steaming in the opposite direction.

22

A New Home

Pearl gazed up at the Statue of Liberty as the *Carpathia* sailed past it. The green copper shone in the spotlights that lit it up in the night sky. She had never been to the Statue of Liberty; she had hardly ventured out of Manhattan at all. Getting to see the monument when it had been practically new was truly an amazing opportunity.

Three long, grueling days had passed since they had said goodbye to *Titanic*'s debris site. Widows had grieved, families had wept, officers had mourned and children had cried as they prepared themselves to deal with the aftermath of the most horrible tragedy of their lives. The days were spent comforting and consoling each other while the nights were filled with sleepless observation. Most survivors did not sleep, for fear of the nightmares that were sure to come.

The passengers of the *Carpathia* were kind and compassionate to the survivors. They offered sleeping quarters and belongings, such as soap and coats. The crew of the *Carpathia* kept the survivors fed and well looked after, giving up empty cabins and stocked-up food. Although more than two-thirds of the people onboard the *Titanic* had died, the crew of the *Carpathia* was doing all they could to help the survivors.

"Can I get your name, miss?"

Pearl turned to see a man with a roster in his hands. Of course, she should have seen this coming. They were taking a list of the survivors to determine the deceased.

Dawson...Rose Dawson...[9] Pearl thought about telling the officer in a moment of whimsical fancy.

Pearl smiled as she replied, "I have already had my name taken."

The man thanked her and moved on to another passenger. Pearl knew there was no way that they did not ask several people twice, what with seven hundred people to go through. Naturally, Pearl could wave him off without causing suspicion.

As Pearl's gaze swept across the deck, she spotted Cecily by the railing, cradling Sean to her chest. Pearl headed over towards her.

"Cecily," Pearl called as she approached her.

Cecily turned to face her. "Pearl. So nice to see you."

"You, too," said Pearl. She gazed down at the baby. "So, did you find out who he is?"

"I don't really know," Cecily told her. "I don't recognize him from the voyage. Do you know who his parents were? You did find him."

---

[9] From James Cameron's *Titanic.*

Pearl sadly shook her head. She suddenly stopped herself, realization hitting her like that iceberg.

Wait a minute, Pearl thought. *No one else was around to see Constance put him in the suitcase. Who is supposed to start the legend if I don't?*

"Well, now that you mention it, he does look familiar," Pearl speculated, putting a finger to her chin and pretending to think. "I believe I saw a couple with him on the ship as they were loading the last lifeboats. They said their name was Dunleavy. Um...Lawrence and Catherine, I believe? No! It was Lachlan and Constance." She frowned once more. "But I could be wrong."

"Well, how did he get in the suitcase?" asked Cecily in wonder.

"I'm not sure," said Pearl, frowning some more for effect. "Maybe she put him in the suitcase when it was floating on the surface."

"Maybe," contemplated Cecily. Her eyes fell to the deck in sorrow. "I'm not even sure which class he is."

"Where's the suitcase?" asked Pearl.

"Um...right over here," said Cecily, leading Pearl to the suitcase twenty feet away.

Pearl smiled as she placed a hand on the water-logged leather. Inside, the three items lay on the floor of the trunk.

"It looks like it belongs to a third-class woman," Pearl told her.

"I think you are right," mused Cecily. "I believe he is an orphan now."

"You are probably right," Pearl said. "There's an orphanage on Seventeenth Street. Highly recommended. Charion United."

"Really? Thank you, Pearl. I'll take him by there as soon as we dock."

"You might want to take the suitcase with you. It could help someone find out who his family was."

"I will," Cecily told her, smiling. "Good luck."

"And to you, as well," Pearl responded, leaving Cecily with her thoughts and her charge.

~~

Pearl stood at the railing of the *Carpathia* with her glasses on, watching as they neared the dock. The passengers were all gathered on the decks, watching and waiting as they finally made port.

On the dock, reporters, family members and random observers waited for the passengers to disembark. As the *Carpathia* anchored and docked, the passengers onboard waited to climb down the gangplanks.

Pearl waited at the back of the crowd, watching as the survivors headed down the gangplank and onto the dock. Margaret Brown walked resolutely into the crowd below. Charles Lightoller gravely strode through the people on the dock.

One by one, the passengers of the *Titanic* disembarked the *Carpathia*, overwhelmed with a combination of relief at having lived through that horrible night, sorrow for those that were lost and blind shock at what had happened so suddenly early on that fateful day.

Pearl moved forward, bringing up the last of the small crowd. She stepped onto the gangplank, easing herself carefully down the steep ramp. As her feet touched solid ground, she felt as though her knees would give out from under her. She was among the few to make it to America; there were many that would never get to walk these steps in this new country.

Pearl looked out at the Atlantic Ocean, gazing past the *Carpathia* and the dark harbor.

About seven hundred miles to the east, the *Titanic* had found her watery grave bed on the floor of the Atlantic. What a strange sight it must be down there. The wreck of the *Titanic* is only known in its later state...covered in rust and silt and barnacles. Right now, the *Titanic* sat on the seabed, new and bright.

The *Titanic* had touched so many people's lives over the years, creating her own legacy. Many were not sure why the story intrigued and fascinated them, but Pearl understood. The sinking of the world's greatest liner had occurred as a result of a set of circumstances that have never happened before, nor will ever happen again.[10]

The *Titanic* may be buried at the bottom of an ocean, but it is the people mesmerized by her story that keep her alive. In the minds and hearts of her enthusiasts, *Titanic* still sails on.

---

[10] From Charles Lightoller's biographical account.

23

William Becomes Sean

Pearl spotted a familiar figure ahead of her, trying to drag a suitcase with one hand and carry a baby with her other hand. Pearl rushed forward, grabbing the suitcase.

"Let me help you with that," said Pearl.

"Oh, it's all right," said Cecily. "I'm sure you have family to get to."

"No, I don't," Pearl assured her. "My husband Samuel is waiting for me back home in Chicago. I will be arriving by train, and it doesn't leave until tomorrow."

"Okay," said Cecily. "Thank you."

Cecily held the baby close in her arms as Pearl grabbed the handle of the trunk to drag it along behind them.

"You wouldn't happen to know where this orphanage is, would you?" asked Cecily.

Pearl looked around at the buildings near them, trying to make out familiar features in the darkness and earlier decade. "I believe it's this way." She pointed down the street to their left.

Together, the three of them headed down the sidewalk towards the orphanage.

"Well..." began Cecily, "tell me about yourself."

"Oh, well..." thought Pearl, "I have a husband named Sam—"

"I already know that," laughed Cecily. "Tell me something else."

"Let's see..." said Pearl, thinking up a cover story. "Samuel and I have a daughter. She's three years old."

"What's her name?" asked Cecily.

Pearl looked back at the *Carpathia*, thinking of all that the *Titanic* represented.

"April," Pearl answered.

Now that Pearl said it out loud, she knew that she would be naming her first daughter April in honor of her ancestors that died on April 15.

"April," pondered Cecily. "That's a very unique name. It's beautiful."

"Thank you. And, well, you know about Samuel's job."

"Oh, yes. The history agency, correct?" asked Cecily.

Pearl nodded.

"What do you do in your spare time?" Cecily wondered.

"I help Sam. I just love history. What about you? Do you have anything that you do?"

"I'm..." began Cecily, seeming to ponder her answer, "an entrepreneur, if you will."

Pearl raised her eyebrows in interest. "Well, now I'm intrigued."

"I create ideas for various things," Cecily explained. "You might even call me an inventor of sorts."

"An inventor?" said Pearl, smiling. "That sounds fun."

"It is," said Cecily. "I came to America to try my newest idea."

"What is it?"

"Accuracy of historical records," Cecily replied.

Pearl looked over at her, stunned.

"It seems as though we're in the same line of work," Cecily proclaimed.

"And what is your revolutionary idea?"

Cecily shook her head slightly, cradling Sean close to her. "It is foolish."

"No, tell me," Pearl pleaded. "I want to know."

Cecily took a deep breath. "Time travel."

Pearl froze in mid-step, staring at Cecily.

Cecily stopped also, watching Pearl. "I know. It's preposterous."

"Actually, it sounds quite extraordinary," Pearl told her as they resumed their walk. "How does it work?"

"Well, I haven't really worked through the details yet, but…it will probably involve electricity, water and copper. Electricity is conducted through the water and copper, and it can be used to…" Cecily trailed off as Pearl stared at her with a smile. "What is it?"

"Oh, nothing," said Pearl. She glanced down at the pavement and back up at Cecily. "You wouldn't happen to know someone with the last name of Tristan, would you?"

"I believe I have a distant cousin with that surname. Why?"

"No reason," Pearl muttered.

So now the truth came out.

Kyle had mentioned that he found the time travel notes buried in his family's old records and filled in the gaps with his own inventions to complete the time machine. He just never knew who had written the notes in the first place. Apparently, not only was he related to her grandfather's savior, but that savior was the basis of why she was here in the first place.

"Is this it?" asked Cecily.

Pearl shook herself out of her thoughts and looked up at the familiar building that was labeled with a sign over the doorway that read, "Charion United."

The building had aged remarkably well. It looked practically the same as it did in 2005—minus one building restoration.

"Yes, this is it," Pearl confirmed. "Do you want me to come in with you?"

Pearl knew she had to accompany Cecily inside so Elizabeth could get a good look at her. She needed to be able to remember that Elizabeth thought she looked like…well, herself, so she would help Sean when she realized it was herself that—

Okay, just stop right now, Pearl thought. *You're gonna give yourself another headache.*

"If you could just bring the suitcase inside for me, I'd appreciate it," said Cecily.

"Of course," said Pearl.

The two women walked into the orphanage, heading over to the front desk. A woman stood at the desk, dressed in a black cotton dress with a white apron.

"How may I help you?" she asked.

"My name is Cecily Miles. I was on the *Titanic*, and we found this little boy in a floating suitcase."

"Oh," said the woman, face drawing a frown.

"Here's the suitcase," Pearl said as she set it on the floor next to Cecily. "Be sure to take it to the White Star Line offices so they can determine who it belongs to."

Pearl knew that the luggage collected in the water in a week's time would be placed on the dock where the *Carpathia* had docked, letting the passengers and families claim what was theirs. This suitcase, however, was never claimed, and therefore, went to the *Titanic* archives. The suitcase needed to make it back to the dock after the photograph of Cecily, Sean and the trunk was taken. The photograph needed to have the suitcase in it so Pearl would see it in 2005 and put the pieces together.

"I will," said Cecily. "Thank you, Pearl." She gave Pearl a brief hug. "I wish you and your family well."

"Thank you," Pearl told her as she stepped away from Cecily. "And good luck on your invention." She looked back down at her infant grandfather one last time. "Goodbye."

Pearl began to walk out of the building when a woman called out. "Elizabeth!"

Pearl turned and saw a little girl at the doorway, staring at her.

Elizabeth Vandez... Pearl realized.

A woman walked up behind Elizabeth and took her back to her room.

Pearl smiled and headed for the door. She exited the orphanage and turned the corner into the alley. She pulled her pendant out of the pouch on the inside of her dress and looked both ways to make sure no one was around. Pearl placed it between both of her thumbs and closed her eyes.

"Take me home," Pearl whispered.

She pressed both thumbs onto the metal and smiled as a white energy enveloped her, jolting her out of the space-time continuum.

Sam...

24

Return to 2005

Pearl hit the floor of the chamber, bedraggled and tired. She sat there for several moments, breathing deeply. She heard a door swinging open and hurried footsteps rushing up to the platform. Someone grabbed onto her shoulders, and Pearl looked up into Sam's face. He was gazing into her eyes, looking very worried.

"Are you okay?" Sam inquired.

Pearl nodded and was immediately enveloped by Sam's arms.

"I was so afraid you wouldn't come back," Sam told her.

Pearl hugged him back, letting him know she was there. They stayed that way for a moment, cherishing this moment. Sam let her go and looked into her eyes once more.

"Where'd you come from?" Sam asked.

"I stayed until the *Carpathia* brought me to New York," Pearl told him. "I just came from the orphanage where Cecily took Sean."

Sam nodded, empathizing with her. "You stayed for the whole thing."

"Yes," Pearl replied.

Sam leaned a little closer, as though it were a secret between the two of them. "Did you see them?"

Pearl knew he was referring to Lachlan and Constance. "Yes, it's true. They were there. I saw them."

Sam smiled. "I'm glad you finally found them." He looked up at their friends in the room. "Let's get you home."

Sam grabbed Pearl's pendant and helped her up. As they neared the doorway, he tossed the pendant into the tray on the desk.

Pearl looked around the observation room as Sam ushered her out. Kyle nodded at her, sending her his silent thanks. Katrina let a tear fall down her face as she took in Pearl's washed-up state. Pearl's dress was rumpled, and her hair was matted down against her head.

Pearl searched through the small crowd, looking for a specific person. Her grandfather's face sprang out from the group, watching her warily. Pearl broke free from Sam's arms and threw herself at her grandfather, hugging him.

"I saved you..." said Pearl. "I saved you..."

"What?" asked Sean.

Pearl pulled away and looked her grandfather in the face. At this point, the entire room was listening intently.

"The woman that brought the suitcase to Cecily's boat...it was me," Pearl announced.

Sean smiled. "It was?"

Pearl nodded.

"What did I tell you about meddling, young lady?" Kyle told her.

Everyone in the room politely laughed.

Pearl smiled up at her grandfather, chuckling a little. "I, like, just left you with Cecily at the orphanage. You grew up fast, boy."

Sean laughed as he hugged Pearl again. "Thank you."

"You're welcome, William."

Sean broke away, frowning at her.

"That was the name that your birth parents gave you: William Dunleavy," Pearl told him.

Her grandfather smiled. "I think I'll stick with Sean."

"Sounds good to me," said Pearl. She let go of Sean and let Sam lead her out the door.

Sam ushered Pearl through the office towards the parking lot. He eased a shaking Pearl into the passenger seat of his Challenger while her family headed to their separate homes, giving Pearl some space. Sam hopped into the driver's seat, starting up the car and heading towards Pearl's house.

Pearl shivered in her seat, whether from the residual cold or the haunting memories, Sam could not tell. Sam gently reached over and wrapped an arm around her shoulder, pulling her towards him across the console. Pearl curled into Sam's side, seeking refuge in the safety of his presence. Sam held her tight, willing her horrible memories to fade into peace and comfort.

Sam could remember how wrecked he was upon his return. It had taken two weeks to fully recover from the trauma, and that included a couple therapy sessions. The process seemed to take years, and Sam sincerely prayed the recovery would not be as long or as painful for Pearl.

Sam parked in Pearl's driveway, pulling her into his arms without a word. He carried her to the front door, unlocking it with the key Pearl had given him that morning in the time lab. He walked over the threshold, closing the door and heading for the stairs. Reaching the second floor, Sam headed around the staircase to his left, approaching the master bedroom door on his right. He nudged the bedroom door open with his foot and took Pearl to the adjoining bathroom.

"You think you can change out of that?" Sam asked her, setting her down on her feet.

"Yeah," Pearl answered timidly.

Sam closed the door and made his way to the closet. He pulled a pair of plaid cotton pants from a drawer and an oversized black T-shirt from a hanger. Knocking on the bathroom door, Sam waited for Pearl to pull it open a crack before handing her the bundle of clothes.

Five minutes later, Pearl exited the bathroom.

"Go ahead and rest," Sam told her, motioning to her bed. "I'll be downstairs." He turned and took a step towards the door.

"Wait," Pearl spoke up.

Sam stopped and looked back at her.

"Will you…" began Pearl.

Pearl did not think she would last if she was left alone…not after the week she'd had. She needed someone to anchor her to this time and place.

Luckily, Sam understood exactly what she was asking. They were so close that they often finished each other's thoughts.

Sam smiled softly, nodding. "Of course."

Pearl settled under her covers as Sam toed his boots off. He pulled the covers back and slid in next to Pearl. As he held his arms open, Pearl snuggled close to his chest, her ear planted above his heart.

As Sam circled his arms around her, Pearl smiled at the sound of his strong, steady heartbeat and the rise and fall of his chest. Here was proof that life still existed after the tragedy the world had endured so long ago.

"You will always be my beautiful pearl," Sam whispered into Pearl's hair.

Pearl smiled as the long overdue sleep clouded through her mind, dragging her off to a world of hopeful wishes and fairytale endings.

25

New Life

Pearl opened her eyes to find herself alone in the bedroom. She looked over at her nightstand. A single red rose was lying next to the locket Sam had given her.

Pearl smiled as she sat up. There was a wonderful smell wafting through the doorway, and she could hear someone moving around in the kitchen.

Pearl climbed out of bed and headed for the stairs. She went downstairs, turned down the hallway between the stairs and the living room, and found Sam in the kitchen.

"You're cooking me breakfast?" Pearl asked as she leaned against the door frame.

"Well, I figured you'd been through enough of an ordeal to last you for a week," Sam said as Pearl sat at the kitchen island on a stool.

Pearl shrugged. "True. Thank you."

"No problem," Sam said with a smile.

A single drumbeat echoed from Sam's pocket.

"Oh, mama, I'm in fear for my life from the long arm of the law!"

Sam reached into his pocket for his cell phone, which was playing Styx's "Renegade." Drumbeats sounded continuously every two beats.

"Hangman is coming down from the gallows, and I don't have very long!"

Sam checked the Caller ID and raised his thumb to answer it as the instruments started in once again.

"Wait!" Pearl told him. "I love this song!"

Sam chuckled, but humored her and waited.

"The jig is up! The news is out! They finally found me! The renegade who had it made, retrieved for the bounty! Nevermore to go astray! This'll be the end today of the wanted man!"

Pearl smiled as she looked at Sam. It was such a relief to hear something familiar, something from her life that never changed.

"Okay, you can answer it now," Pearl said.

Sam laughed as he answered the call. "Hello?" He listened for a moment. "Yeah, she's doing great. Slept in for a while."

Sam nodded, although the person on the other end could not see him.

"Okay, will do," he concluded and hung up.

"Who was that?" asked Pearl.

"Kyle," Sam answered. "He wanted to know how you were." He turned toward Pearl. "Well, what do you think: coffee or tea?"

"Neither," Pearl said.

Sam looked at her.

"You know what sounds really good?" Pearl proposed.

Sam stared at her, confused.

"Apple juice," Pearl told him.

Pearl smiled as Sam started laughing. She laughed with him as he went to the cabinet and grabbed a glass. He walked over to the fridge and pushed the lever for the ice machine. As two ice cubes slid into the glass, they made a clinking sound that halted Pearl's laugh.

She closed her eyes as memories flooded her mind: an iceberg looming out of the darkness, the terrible scraping sound as the starboard hull was pierced, water flooding the decks as they sank, people screaming as they jumped to their deaths, the explosion of rivets and iron as the ship broke in two, the stern plunging under the surface, and the cries of the condemned floating over the seas that still night.

Pearl opened her eyes and stared at the innocent ice cubes, amazed at how they could bring back so many memories.

Sam followed her gaze and walked over to dump the ice into the sink.

"I know it must be ridiculous—" Pearl began.

"No, it's all right," Sam told her. "I know what it's like. After I came back, I would practically hit the deck any time I heard what even remotely sounded like gunfire."

Pearl held up her hand and looked at it, lost in thought. Sam came over and sat down on the stool next to her. Pearl looked at him.

"I touched it," Pearl confided in him. "I touched the iceberg as it passed on the starboard side that night. And it…"

"It made it more real," Sam finished.

Pearl nodded.

"I know this won't make you feel better, but...there was nothing you could've done," Sam reassured her. "Even if you had changed history and warned Murdoch about the iceberg that night, they still probably couldn't have turned fast enough."

Pearl narrowed her eyes at him, wondering how he could have known.

"Oh, come on," said Sam, interpreting Pearl's look. "I know you all too well."

Pearl smiled, nodding. "Well, you're right about that."

Sam let the smile fade slowly from his face, looking down at his hands. "Well, it's still true." He looked up into her face. "There was nothing you could do. The rudder was too small. The *Titanic* was doomed from the day it was launched."

Pearl looked up at him. "You remember the dream I kept having before I went? About dying on the *Titanic*?"

Sam nodded.

"I was living it," Pearl confessed. "I was starting to relive it. But then I grabbed the locket you gave me, and I knew I had to get back to you. And, in that moment, it was as though you were reaching through time for me. I suddenly found a way to survive."

"Glad I could help," Sam said with a smile. "So, how was it? I mean, the whole...you know."

Pearl looked him in the eyes, thinking. "James Cameron got it...pretty close."

Sam nodded, thinking about that. "A true visionary, huh?"

Pearl laughed as Sam smiled.

Sam looked at his hands as Pearl's laughter died down. "I found a note on the table next to the door…the goodbye note."

Pearl's smile faded as she froze. It seemed like a lifetime ago that she had written that letter, when in reality, it was technically only twenty-four hours ago.

"Did you mean it?" Sam asked.

Pearl hesitated for a second. "Well, I *was* headed for the *Titanic*." She took a deep breath, trying to figure everything out. "Before I left…in the time lab…there was something you said that—"

"Well, I didn't want you to go without saying it."

"Right," said Pearl, leaning back a little and relaxing in her chair. "You didn't know if you'd ever see me again. People say things they don't mean."

"Who says I didn't mean it?" Sam told her.

Pearl stared at him, transfixed by the sincere look in his eyes. She smiled at him, searching for a way to break the ice…figuratively speaking. Sam's eyes shifted to the front door and back to Pearl.

"Would you like to go for a walk?" Sam offered.

Pearl smiled, snatching onto the subject change. "I'd love to."

The two of them headed to the front door with Sam leading the way.

"So, your morning looking a little better?" Sam asked her, reaching for the knob of the front door and turning it.

Pearl shrugged. "I guess so."

"Well, I know what will make it a whole lot better," Sam told her as he held the door open for her.

"Oh, really?" Pearl speculated as she walked out the door, still looking at Sam. "And what would that be?"

Pearl turned toward the street as she finished her question, and her jaw dropped as she froze on the spot.

"Surprise!" cried six voices from the street.

Her six other friends stood at the curb in front of her house around a royal blue classic Chevrolet Impala with a giant red bow sitting on top of the roof.

"No…way…" Pearl breathed, running up to the car.

The Impala's blue skin shone in the sun, polished perfectly. The chrome around the windows, fender and taillights reflected exactly like a mirror. The black leather upholstery curved over the front and back seats. The cream-colored interior of the doors and dashboard held not a scratch or a scuff. The blue beauty looked "brand-spankin'-new." Pearl could just imagine AC/DC's "Highway to Hell" playing as she examined the muscle car.

Pearl looked up at Sam, who had joined the group. "'67?"

"Yep," said Sam. "327 four barrel, 475 horses…They don't make them any better than this."

Pearl's gaze flew back to the car as she walked around it. "How?"

"We had a little extra money from the *Titanic* project," Rose told her. She shrugged as she frowned a little. "Well, okay, a lot more. And we figured this could pass for getting paid for the trip."

"But we haven't even presented the data to that museum guy yet," Pearl said as she continued to admire the car.

"He paid us up front," Kyle told her. "He insisted."

Pearl reached the driver's side of the hood, running a reverent hand along the metal.

"Would you like us to leave you two alone?" asked Chris.

Pearl looked up at him and laughed. "That'd be great. Scram."

The others laughed as Pearl walked to the front fender, staring in awe at her new car.

"Yur itchin' to drive 'er, aren't ya?" Connor asked, holding up a set of keys.

Pearl smiled as Connor tossed the keys to her. She caught them and hurried to the driver's door. As she unlocked the door and climbed inside, Katrina and Mary took the bow off of the top.

Pearl put the key into the ignition and turned it. She smiled as the engine purred to life, humming through the frame.

Pearl leaned over, rolled the passenger window down, and looked at Sam. "Want a ride?"

Sam grinned. "Oh, you know it."

Sam climbed into the passenger seat, and Pearl peeled away from the curb, turning on a classic rock station. Bobbing their heads to Billy Squier's "Lonely Is the Night," Sam and Pearl drove through the city, their breakfast completely forgotten.

~~

Pearl sat in her study later that day, going through a book about the wreck of the *Titanic*. She came across a page that showed a white doll head lying on the ocean floor. She froze when she saw that image: she had seen a child in first-class carrying one of those porcelain lady dolls.

Pearl began flipping through the book, noticing familiar objects: the crusted windows of the first-class lounge, the statuette from the mantelpiece of the first-class lounge submerged in the mud, a twisted section of the descending balustrade from the grand staircase half-buried in the mud, a shattered fragment of the leaded glass windows from the first-class dining saloon, the barnacle-encrusted falls hanging from the empty lifeboat davits, a pair of shoes lying side-by-side on the ocean floor...

Many images such as these gazed up from the pages of the book, providing a shocking reminder of the reality of what had transpired those six days nearly a hundred years ago. Debris that was once décor, treasures turned tarnished, magnificence made memories...

These riches and belongings had all been very used at one point, giving a sense of ghosts among the wreckage. If she listened close enough, she could almost hear the phantom cries of the passengers drifting out of the pages in front of her.

Pearl placed a hand to her mouth as the tears sprang to her eyes. She had seen these artifacts in person, had watched the passengers and crew use these very objects, had even touched many of the ghostly treasures now buried under thirteen thousand feet of water.

This is not how I remember it... Pearl thought, shaking her head.

When people thought about the *Titanic*, they imagined it was a dream long since passed, an urban legend told from generation to generation. And why shouldn't they? The only evidence they have of the story was a twisted, disintegrating wreck at the bottom of the ocean. It looked nothing like this fabled ship of historical legend. It was hard to imagine that the two were one and the same.

Pearl turned the page, seeing a picture of the bow of the *Titanic* sitting in a hazy fog of ocean. *Titanic* sat in solitude on the ocean floor, a lone, eerie reminder of that awful day. Although the ship would never be as magnificent as she once was, the wrecked *Titanic* held a stark beauty of its own: the ship standing tall and proud on the ocean floor, kicking up a bow wave in the mud. It was certainly an awe-inspiring sight, seeing that image of the *Titanic* alive again.[11] Nearly a hundred years buried at sea and still determined to survive.

Pearl felt tears fall down her face as she stared at the picture.

"Are you all right?"

Pearl looked up at Sam, who stood in the doorway of the study. Pearl glanced back at the book and slowly shook her head. Sam walked over to Pearl, spotting the book open on her desk to a page that showed the dark, hazy bow covered in rust.

Sam sighed and wheeled Pearl's chair over to the small couch along the wall. Sam sat on the couch, positioning the chair in front of him. He moved his hands to Pearl's shoulders, and Pearl leaned into his embrace, circling her arms around him. Sam rubbed soothing hands on her back, letting her take whatever comfort she needed.

After a moment, Pearl eased away from Sam, looking into his face. Sam smiled calmly at her, letting her know silently that everything would be okay. Their faces were only a few inches apart, and they gazed into each other's eyes, connecting with one another.

---

[11] From Robert Ballard's account.

Sam was the first to move, slowly leaning his head forward towards her own. Pearl returned the gesture until their lips touched in an intimate display of passion. The kiss felt excitingly novel and enticingly thrilling. The secret lovers were rediscovering each other in the most special way possible, reassessing their relationship. Pearl felt her stomach muscles flutter under her skin, taking her breath away.

Pearl and Sam pulled away from each other, both stunned into silence. They opened their eyes and looked into each other's gaze, letting smiles break out upon their faces.

"Well, that was new," murmured Pearl.

Sam huffed out a small laugh. "It certainly was." He reached a hand forward and placed it against her cheek, wiping his thumb across her skin to remove her faded tears. "Question is...does it change anything?"

Pearl smiled as she covered his hand with hers. "Definitely."

They leaned towards each other and resumed their kiss.

Epilogue

Three years later
2008

As Pearl and Sam exited the final exhibit room, they handed their audio devices to a steward in period servant dress.

They had just finished their tour of the *Titanic* museum in Branson, Missouri, and they had really enjoyed it...probably due to the fact that Pearl had been the inspiration for the whole thing.

Sam and Pearl stepped toward the second-floor railing of the replica of the grand staircase, leaning on it as the music from the movie "*Titanic*" echoed around the room from the speakers.

"So...bring back memories?" Sam asked her.

"More than I thought it would," Pearl told him as she wiped a tear from her eye.

Sam took Pearl's hands in his own and kissed her cheek. "It really is a beautiful museum. Thank you."

Sam stepped up behind Pearl, wrapping his arms around her as they enjoyed the view.

Pearl's eyes shone at the intricate detailing done to convey the grandeur of first-class. It looked exactly like it had on the ship, each splinter of wood, scrap of gold, shard of glass and bar of metal in place and brand new.

Pearl gazed up at the glass dome that illuminated the room, smiling as she listened to the beautiful music. The music swelled to a crescendo, and Pearl's entire being seemed to swell with it.

This room would always hold a special place in her heart, in more ways than one. Not only was it her favorite room on the ship, but it was where she and Sam had exchanged vows.

~~

One year previously

Pearl straightened the veil hanging from her hair as her friends and family stood around her.

She was standing in the Father Browne exhibit room of the *Titanic* museum in Branson, Missouri. Authentic photographs taken by Father Francis M. Browne onboard the *Titanic* while traveling from Southampton to Queenstown surrounded the wedding party.

Pearl looked around at her bridesmaids. Rose, Katrina and Mary were dressed in full-length sapphire satin dresses that were spaghetti-strapped and had an open back. The bottom of the dresses flowed around their ankles. Pearl's maid of honor, her sister Tru, was dressed the same way.

Sam's groomsmen and best man wore tuxedos with scarlet-colored ties and gray vests. Kyle, Connor and Chris stood awaiting the ceremony. Sam's brother Tobias was the best man for the day, and he was with Sam and the priest, waiting to start the ceremony.

Pearl's sister currently stood at the doorway to the corridor, talking with Connor. Connor laughed as Tru did also, placing her hand on his shoulder.

Well, looks like Tru found her Texas man, thought Pearl.

Pearl's grandfather Sean stood in the corner, smiling at Pearl.

Pearl walked over to her grandfather. "Hi."

"Hey," said Sean, smiling. "You look so beautiful. Your father would have been so proud."

"Thanks," said Pearl. She looked over at her wedding planner as she walked into the room.

"Okay," the wedding planner stated. "We have a little over a minute to go. Good luck, everyone."

Pearl smiled as she looked around at the wedding party.

She and Sam had decided to get married on the grand staircase in the *Titanic* museum on April 15, 2007—the ninety-fifth anniversary of the disaster. The guests currently sat on the landing in front of the staircase, waiting for the ceremony to start and listening to the music they had selected for the waiting period.

As Pearl listened, the music ended, and some soft music began playing. The bridesmaids joined their groomsmen companions and lined up to begin the procession.

Pearl's brother John held an arm out for Sam's grandmother. John ushered Janice through the winding third-class corridor and into the grand staircase.

Pearl's brother Leo held his arm out for their grandmother Kate and ushered her out into the audience.

John then returned to usher their mother Helen to her seat.

Rose and Connor locked arms with Rose straightening her white iris bouquet. As they proceeded out of the corridor and down the aisle, Katrina and Kyle locked arms and proceeded down the hallway. Chris and Mary next walked down the corridor before Tru turned towards the hallway.

Pearl walked over to Sean, nervous.

"It's time," said Sean.

"Thank you for everything," said Pearl.

"Oh, no," said Sean. "Thank you." He looked around at the room. "After all, without you, this place wouldn't have been possible."

Pearl smiled as Sean held his arm out for her. She laced her arm through his as they turned towards the corridor.

The music changed to the wedding march, "Canon in D," and Pearl and Sean made their way through the corridor. They passed a model of a third-class berth on their left, and exhibits of silverware and trinkets on their right. They turned to their left, winding with the corridor and coming to a dog kennel door on their right. They turned to their left once again, approaching the entryway to the grand staircase. Pearl and Sean turned to their right and entered the staircase room.

The audience was standing up, looking towards Pearl as she entered. Pearl smiled as she walked into the grand staircase room, glancing at the landing of the Honor and Glory clock.

Sam and the priest were standing in front of the clock at the top of the stairs. On the right side of the staircase, the groomsmen stood along the railing with Tobias at the top and Connor at the bottom. On the left, the bridesmaids stood with Tru at the top and Rose at the bottom.

Pearl walked along the back of the room, turning when they reached the aisle. They made their way down the aisle, heading for the staircase. Sam walked down to join them at the bottom and stood on Pearl's other side. The three of them looked up at the priest.

"Dearly beloved, we are gathered here today in the presence of these witnesses to join Sam and Pearl in the bonds of holy matrimony," said the priest. "In the years they have been together, their love and understanding of each other has grown and matured, and now they have decided to live their lives together as husband and wife. If any person can show just cause as to why these two may not be joined together, let them speak now or forever hold their peace."

The priest paused for the customary silence before turning towards Sean and Pearl.

"Who gives this woman to this man?" asked the priest.

"Her family," said Sean.

He hugged Pearl, kissing her on the cheek, and turned to sit with Kate in the audience.

Sam took Pearl by the arm and led her up the staircase to the landing. Pearl faced the priest with Sam as they joined hands next to each other.

"Love is a bond that transcends time," recited the priest. "It reaches through the timeless bonds of space to touch those that we are close to. It saves us when we think there is no hope left to be saved. It is this love that has brought this man and this woman together today."

Pearl and Sam smiled as the priest continued with his reading.

"The following is a passage called 'On Love' by Thomas a Kempis," the priest told them. He opened his book and began reciting.

"'Love is a mighty power, a great and complete good. Love alone lightens every burden, and makes rough places smooth. It bears every hardship as though it were nothing, and renders all bitterness sweet and acceptable. Nothing is sweeter than love, nothing stronger, nothing higher, nothing wider, nothing more pleasant, nothing fuller or better in heaven or earth; for love is born of God.

"'Love flies, runs and leaps for joy. It is free and unrestrained. Love knows no limits, but ardently transcends all bounds. Love feels no burden, takes no account of toil, attempts things beyond its strength. Love sees nothing as impossible, for it feels able to achieve all things. It is strange and effective, while those who lack love faint and fail. Love is not fickle and sentimental, nor is it intent on vanities. Like a living flame and a burning torch, it surges upward and surely surmounts every obstacle.'"

The priest closed his book and looked at Sam and Pearl. "You may now exchange your vows."

Sam grasped Pearl's hands in his as they turned towards each other. "Pearl…you are the most amazing woman I've ever met. I love your passion for life and your compassion for others. Ever since I saw you…I knew you were the one. Every day when I saw you, I would think, 'I'm gonna to marry that girl some day.' And after your project at work, I knew I wasn't going to let you get away again. Pearl, I am so happy with you in my life, and I want to spend the rest of my life with you."

Pearl felt a single tear slip down her face as Sam finished.

"Sam," Pearl began, "I've never felt this way about anyone before. You were the one that was there for me when I needed you, in good times and bad. You pulled me from my sinking ship and brought me into a world of new beginnings. I've been in love with you longer than I can remember. I couldn't imagine one moment without you. You make me feel like I can fly."

Sam appeared to be a little wet-eyed as Pearl finished. Pearl smiled up at him as the priest turned to Sam.

"Do you have the rings?" asked the priest.

Pearl turned to Tru, who handed the solid gold band to her. Pearl faced Sam again, looking down at the gold ring studded with two lines of small diamonds he now held in his hand.

"Repeat after me," said the priest. "I, Sam…"

"I, Sam…" recited Sam as he took Pearl's left hand in both of his.

"…take thee, Pearl…"

"…take thee, Pearl…"

"…to be my lawfully wedded wife…"

"…to be my lawfully wedded wife…"

"...for better or worse, in sickness and in health, forsaking all others, as long as we both shall live."

"...for better or worse, in sickness and in health, forsaking all others, as long as we both shall live."

Sam slid the ring onto Pearl's ring finger, clasping her hands in front of him. "I give you this ring as an eternal symbol of my love and commitment to you."

The priest turned slightly towards Pearl. "Repeat after me. I, Pearl..."

"I, Pearl..." Pearl replied as she shifted her hands to grasp Sam's left hand.

"...take thee, Sam..."

"...take thee, Sam..."

"...to be my lawfully wedded husband..."

"...to be my lawfully wedded husband..."

"...for better or worse, in sickness and in health, forsaking all others, as long as we both shall live."

"...for better or worse, in sickness and in health, forsaking all others, as long as we both shall live."

Pearl slid the gold band onto Sam's ring finger, smiling as they clasped hands once again. "I give you this ring as an eternal symbol of my love and commitment to you."

They smiled at each other, Sam rubbing his thumb over Pearl's new ring.

"Do you, Samuel Alexander Wyatt, take Pearl Iris Liberti, to be your wife, to have and to hold from this day forth until death do you part?" asked the priest.

"I do," Sam said.

"Do you, Pearl Iris Liberti, take Samuel Alexander Wyatt, to be your husband, to have and to hold from this day forth until death do you part?"

Pearl smiled, her vision blurring as she began tearing up again. "I do."

The priest placed his hands on top of their clasped hands. "May your joys be as bright as the morning, your years of happiness as numerous as the stars in the heavens, and your troubles but shadows that fade in the sunlight of love."

The priest removed his hands, holding his book in front of him.

"By the power vested in me by the State of Missouri, I now pronounce you man and wife," said the priest. "You may kiss the bride."

Sam placed his hands gently on either side of Pearl's face, his palms cupping her ears. Pearl leaned her face up as Sam leaned his down, meeting in the middle in a passionate kiss.

The audience applauded as Sam and Pearl shared their first kiss as husband and wife. As they broke apart, they turned towards the small audience assembled at the bottom of the stairs.

"It's my pleasure to present to you…Mr. and Mrs. Samuel Wyatt," the priest announced.

The audience applauded as Pearl took Sam's arm, and they made their way down the stairs. The newlyweds walked down the aisle towards the third-class corridor as people stood for them.

"You were right, Pearl," Sam whispered as he looked up at the glass dome above them. "It's beautiful."

Sam and Pearl smiled at each other as they entered the third-class corridor, passing by an exhibit of a certain suitcase found floating among the debris, the only items inside being a purse, a bracelet and a blue dress jacket. Pearl looked back at Sam, giving him a radiant smile as they walked through the third-class corridor towards the Father Browne exhibit.

~~

Present
2008

Pearl smiled as she gazed around the grand staircase, marveling in its beauty and magnificence. Her gaze roamed the twinkling-glass chandelier, the marble-linoleum stairs and the polished-oak banisters, coming to rest on an exhibit across the room on the first floor in the third-class corridor. The exhibit held the suitcase that had been left on the dock in New York after Cecily brought it to the White Star Line offices.

Pearl let her memory wander back to the celebrated liner as she gazed at what had been her grandfather's home for a few brief moments that night ninety-six years ago.

A female employee dressed as a stewardess stepped up next to Pearl and Sam at the railing.

"It's amazing, isn't it?" the woman commented, looking up at the beautiful glass dome as she smiled. "It makes you feel like you're actually there."

Pearl glanced up at Sam, and they shared a secret smile. Pearl gazed back down at the room, snuggling closer into her husband's embrace.

"Yeah," said Pearl as she recalled the five unforgettable days onboard almost three years previously. "It does."

Pearl admired their surroundings, which looked exactly like the real thing. She smiled at the thought of the museum and the enthusiasts yet to visit.

Indeed, the *Titanic* still sails on.

Appendix

All historical research completed for this novel, including any mention of historical incidents, taken from the following books and movies:

Ballard, Robert, and Rick Archbold. *Titanic.* Toronto, Ontario: Madison Press, 2007.

Ghosts of the Abyss. Dir. James Cameron. Walt Disney, 2003. Documentary.

Green, Rod. *Building the Titanic: An Epic Tale of the Creation of History's Most Famous Ocean Liner.* Pleasantville, New York: Reader's Digest, 2005.

Merideth, Lee W. *Titanic Names: A Complete List of the Passengers and Crew.* 2nd ed. Sunnyvale, CA: Rocklin Press, 2007.

Tibballs, Geoff. *The Titanic: The Extraordinary Story of the Unsinkable Ship.* Pleasantville, New York: Reader's Digest, 1997.

Titanic. Dir. James Cameron. Perf. Kate Winslet, Leonardo DiCaprio, Billy Zane, Victor Garber, Bernard Hill, Kathy Bates, and Frances Fisher. Paramount, 1997. Film.

Winocour, Jack, ed. *The Story of the Titanic as told by its Survivors.* New York: Dover Publications, Inc., 1960.

Made in the USA
Lexington, KY
25 November 2016